JACQULINE'S CHOICE

MR. NIBS

Illustrated by AMBER ARIA
Cover by SABER-TOOTHED ERMINE
Copyedited by DRAGON & MASKED LIONESS

That broke the spell. Jacqueline's jaw worked and sputtered as she struggled to remember how to make the sounds that made up her name. She looked from the crowd to his handsome face, with sculpted features that could have walked right out of a movie screen, if not for the fact that he was shorter than her own five-five. His almost impossibly blue eyes seemed to radiate warmth and encouragement. Looking into them, Jacqueline felt some of her tension drain away. "My name is Jacqueline," she managed to whisper into the mic.

"Alright, Jacqueline, are you willing to follow my instructions to assist me with this next trick?" His smile seemed to grow even wider as he spoke.

"Uh, sure?"

"Excellent!" Jacqueline felt a dull pain right behind her eyes and for a brief moment there was a sensation of something threading through her brain. A blink and it was gone. She just saw Menzo's warm smile.

The magician slid his attention from her to the crowd with an effortless grace. "Ladies and gentleman!" Jacqueline had to admire the way he did that. While none of the tricks so far had been things she hadn't seen before, Menzo had performed them with such mastery and enthusiasm that you forgot about the fact you knew how half of them worked. They were just an excuse to watch him perform. The audience's attention eagerly slid from her and back to him. "Allow me to present to you, Jacqueline!" There was a pause as he smiled conspiratorially at the crowd, as if he was about to share a great secret with them. "The LLLeoparrrrd LLLLady!" he whispered in a low voice with a hint of a seductive growl as he stretched out the name.

The crowd ooohed as Jacqueline blinked in confusion. "What?" She managed to protest. At the utterance, Menzo's eyes turned back to her, warm showmen's smile transmuting into mischievous grin. Jacqueline wasn't sure if she was being insulted or not. Was "Leopard Lady" some sort of slang she hadn't heard of? Like a cougar or a wildcat? His blue eyes did not contain a hint of insult but there a twinkle of unspoken laughter in them. "I-I'm not a leopard!" She had originally planned to go along with the act, but she felt off balance; this wasn't part of any trick she had seen before. "I-I'm not a leopard!"

"You are spotted like a leopard, are you not?" He snaked his arm around her waist and pressed the side of his hip to hers while making a sweeping gesture with his other hand that caught all the eyes in the room, including Jacqueline's. "Observe," and pointed to Jacqueline's torso where a very tight leopard print tube top clung to her chest.

"Oh." Jacqueline mentally smacked herself. She had totally forgotten about what she was wearing. The girl's night out had been hasty assembled after their husbands had declared it poker night, and she hadn't put a lot of thought into what she grabbed out of her drawers. She had just worn the tightest pair of jeans she could squeeze herself into without causing major discomfort. The tube top was a nice, if tacky, splash of color in between the open front of her white track jacket; together they framed the deep cleavage of her breasts, generous C cups pushed into wow range by her push up bra. Between those puppies on her chest and the jeans shaping her legs into sexy curves, she was worth more than a second glance. Looking in the mirror before she had rushed out to pile into Lucy's car, she had thought she looked cute with a hint of wildness, the bust pushing her into sexy range. Now on stage being compared to a feline, her cheeks flushed, she felt a little childish to be wearing the top; it harked back to her college days, depressingly close to a decade ago. "Um, it's just a top," she managed to say.

Menzo turned back to the crowd, "I think poor Jacqueline's spots have gotten lost on her shirt! Shall we help them home?"

"Yeah!" The crowd roared back, completely enthralled with the performance.

"Just hold still for a moment, Miss Jacqueline," Menzo whispered as he released her and approached the crowd. She watched him with a worried expression as he pulled a white cloth from his sleeve, about two feet square. He presented it to the crowd, showing them that it was indeed white on both sides. Then, grasping the upper corners, he held it in front of Jacqueline's torso, preventing anyone from seeing her tacky top. "Spotifizastic!" He shouted and gave the cloth a quick snap, and Jacqueline flinched as she felt a shiver of wind encircle her midsection. She blinked several times at the cloth held in front of her; it was no longer white, it was a leopard print, identical to the one on her top.

She looked down and gasped, the top was still there, but it was pure white. The crowd cheered as Menzo lowered the now spotted cloth and directed their eyes to Jacqueline. Blinking, Jacqueline ignored the crowd; inspecting the now white top was a much greater priority. Running her hands over the curve of her breast, fingers brushing the seams. It was the same top. She could feel a small hole in the side where a rather drunk frat boy had almost ripped it off her years ago.

Just what was going on here? Real magic was too dangerous for performances, so they said. She looked up at Menzo and found him at the front of the stage, his huge top hat on the floor in front of him as he pantomimed ringing the cloth out over it. A flick and the cloth was open, pure white once again. He stuffed it back into his sleeve with a flourish. Then he picked up the hat very carefully, as if it was full of water, and carried it back to Jacqueline. She looked at him, then at the hat and back at him with growing sense of dread. He smiled, stole a wink back at his audience, and he placed the hat on her head with a flourish.

Something cold flowed out of the hat as soon as it touched Jacqueline's head; the feeling raced down her neck, spreading out across her back. She gasped as it encircled her limbs and flowed across her chest, nipples hardening as if she'd jumped into frigid water. Instinctively, she moved her hands up over her face, pushing her long brown hair behind her head as if surfacing from underwater.

A whisper in her ear, "Jacqueline, take off your jacket." Numbly, she obeyed, shrugging the jacket from her shoulders and then it was quickly whisked from her arms by Menzo's waiting hands. Jacqueline's jaw dropped as her bare arms were revealed, they were covered in small, irregularly shaped spots, leopard spots. She looked over herself; they were on her shoulders, the back of her hands, and particularly large ones on her chest. She pulled at the elastic band of her top to peer down it; the large spots covered her breasts and her stomach in irregular rows.

Menzo's voice shook her from any further exploration, "Now is she or is she not a fine Leopard Lady?" Jacqueline looked up to see him displaying her coat to the crowd like it was a trophy of conquest. That's when she saw them, without his hat they were clear as day; Menzo's ears were not that of a human being. Only one creature she knew of possessed long pointed ears like those, each one nearly three inches long. She was alone on the stage with one of the Fey.

As Menzo strode back towards her, she was thinking about iron. She needed cold iron. All the websites she read about fey advised you not to leave the house without some cold-tempered iron. The touch of it burned them and the pain of it usually drove them off, so

Looking away from her reflection, she found her wedding band on her finger and focused on it, on Dave. "Nnn-No. This isn't real. It's glamour. You're… You're using the crowd to force it on me." There, he'd asked her twice now and she had denied it twice. By the rule of three, he could only ask her once more. She just had to hang on that long.

"Oh, that's what I'm doing, am I? You think this is just another magic trick?" He shook his head sadly. "You poor, lost kitten. What if you're wrong? Perhaps I am not applying glamour to you, but stripping it away instead." He ran a finger down the length of her tail, setting off another shiver. "Think of what you dream about at night, Jacqueline." He stopped administering to her happy spot and passed a hand through her hair in a tender manner, the tips of his fingers just brushing her ear. Her body ached for further touch but he abruptly stood and faced the crowd. "Now, do you like what you see here?"

While the crowd roared their approval, Jacqueline stayed on her hands and knees, frozen, as her mind spinning like a super-sonic merry-go-round. He had just insinuated that she was actually a changeling, but that wasn't possible. Was it? Her parents were normal and she'd been tested for magic. Hell, Dave worked for a company with a strict no-magic policy and he had more magic than she did. No, it must be another trick. And the dreams… Well, didn't everyone have odd dreams once in a while?

Slowly, she pushed herself to her feet, giving herself one last look in the mirror, "You're not real," she told the image of the Leopard Woman that faced her. The reflection did not look convinced. Over the reflection's shoulder, she could see Menzo digging around in his top hat for something. He was clearly filling time, waiting for her. Swallowing, she steeled herself for the next round in this contest over her body. She turned to face him just in time to see him pull out a pair of tribal bongos that were a about four times the size of his hat.

He drummed a quick rhythm on the surface of one the drums with his fingers, just a few beats were enough to send Jacqueline's stomach into a fit of somersaults. There was no way he could know that beat. Menzo's gaze slid back to her, a triumphant grin had spread across his face, his too-white teeth looking positively predatory. "Jacqueline, what did you dream about last night?" Without waiting for an answer, he started to play.

"I-I was dancing."

"Where were you dancing?"

The beat seemed to resonate with her spine and Jacqueline's hips began to respond without asking for approval, swaying back and forth to the slow, steady beat, her tail swaying behind her, exaggerating her hips' sinuous motions. The barely remembered dream bubbled up in her mind. She tried to hold back the words that rose in her throat, to lie, to do anything to avoid admitting that this had been her dream, but the words burst out of her mouth with eagerness. "I was dancing in the jungle, on the edge of a village, around a huge fire."

The beat took hold of her arms then and they lifted over her head to join the motions of her hips swaying to the slow, sensual beat.

"And what were you wearing while you danced, Jacqueline?"

She bit her lip and held her breath as she tried to fight the compulsion that gripped her every time he spoke her name. It worked, but only until her lungs began to burn a few seconds later and the words burst out with the air from her lungs. "I danced naked."

"Dance for us, Jacqueline. Dance the way it's supposed to be danced." He continued to drum the soft beat.

Jacqueline growled at him, trying to ignore her secret thrill that the prospect of dancing naked in front of all these people was causing. It wasn't her fault after all, she was being forced. Forced to show them what lurked in her now ill-fitting clothing. Maybe, just maybe, she could get Menzo distracted enough to make a mistake. Yes, that was it. Her mind seized on that plan and she embraced the dance.

Her body undulated as she moved her torso in a shallow wave traveling from her hips slowly up her spine. She turned her head away from the crowd as she brought a clawed fingertip up to the top of her tube top, right between her deep cleavage. Thrusting her

With nothing left to hold them to her body, they fell away from her. The panties floated down on top of the jeans a second later.

Then she danced for them. Her body moved through the beat with an impossible grace and speed. The fire she circled grew with each step as her mind flooded with feral images, full of the scents of blood and sex. As the beat neared its climax, she reached the point where she could no longer ignore the burning of her own loins. It had made her inner thighs slick with something that was not sweat. Her hands flowed over her spotted skin; they dawdled on her large breasts, cupping them first and then pinching her swollen nipples, their dark brown skin changing to black as she moaned in pleasure. One hand stayed on her breast while the other quested down her spotted stomach and through the curly brown hair of her mons until her fingers met the wet warmth of her dripping pussy. She pressed through its folds and began to stroke her clitoris to the pulse of the beat. All the while, the fire beside her grew.

The dance forgotten, her mouth opened, allowing her tongue to loll out as she began to pant. She squatted down as her other hand slid down from her breasts, along the curve of her body, across the contour of her thigh to plunge a finger inside of her. A roar ripped through her as she pressed the finger against her inner walls. The fire beside her surged, the flames extending above her head. As her hands pulsed in a frenzied rhythm, her head slowly tilted backwards until her face was level with the sky. Her muscular legs ground against her hands with increasing desperation as the beat of the drums reached a dizzying speed.

The fire grew into a roaring bonfire, casting Jacqueline in a lusty red glow that made the sweat on her spotted skin shine as her body shook with ecstasy, her tail trembling behind her. She made stran-gled noise, a blend of human and inhuman, "aaaaarrrriiiii." She came, screaming as her knees gave out and she crashed to the ground.

For a long moment, she just lay there, panting. She did not want to move. The musky scent of her own sex and sweat, and the pop and crackle of the fire beside her, seemed to cast the world into a comfortable twilight. There was a tingling soreness in her, focusing her tired and foggy mind until her attention localized the sensation to an abraded clit. It was sated, but there was longing ache much deeper within her, waiting…

A familiar voice came to her, "Jacqueline, maybe you should clean yourself. You've gotten a little dirty."

Only the briefest of nods answered him. He was right, of course. Fur became a crusty mess if you did not clean it right after sex. Sighing, Jacqueline pulled herself up onto her knees, careful not to let her hands touch the packed earth beneath her anymore than they already had. She brought a hand to her lips and licked it from wrist to fingertip. It felt wrong, the skin too smooth, her tongue too wet. Another lick and things felt better, the tongue rough now on her skin. Skin? She opened her eyes to inspect her hands. They were long-fingered things, their spots looking odd on the yellowish skin. How was she supposed to run on these if she needed an extra burst of speed? As soon as the question was asked, the answer appeared, as a patch of yellow and black hairs grew over the skin she had cleaned with her tongue. As she watched, it thickened into proper fur, assuming the coloration of the skin beneath it. She licked it and her tongue pulled at the fur in the luxurious manner she had expected. Moreover, she could feel the patch of fur grow larger as her tongue passed over it. Murring, she continued to groom her odd paw and, under her administrations, it began to fix itself. As the fur crept over it, her hand thickened, growing wider. Dark, leathery pads rose from her palm as her claws merged with the fingertip bones, becoming fearsome weapons. Painlessly, the claws bent backwards, folding into the flesh of her now-thick fingers and disappearing from view.

The other hand was quickly groomed into a proper hand-paw before Jacqueline pushed herself up onto her toes and opened her legs, wincing as stuck skin peeled away from itself. The brown hair around her sex was shiny with her juices. Like her hands, this also needed correcting. Her supple spine almost allowed her to reach it with her tongue, but not quite. It was yet another thing that she found strange about her body. She growled in frustration and tried again, applying all her considerable will to the movement. Her back resisted at first, then yielded to her desire with a strange slipping sensation as several vertebra lengthened and the accompanying cartilage softened to allow to her questing tongue to lap at her own pussy. On contact with her rough tongue, her curly public hair melted into silky, white fur. Cleaning herself in this way was a relaxing, calming sensation, so she took her time and there was more fur to clean with every stoke. It had coated her inner thighs and was starting to creep up her stomach when the voice interrupted.

"Are you ready for your lesson now, Jacqueline?"

Jacqueline felt her cheeks flush as her tail curled around her ankles in embarrassment. "Sorry, I got a little carried away there."

"Pleasure is an important part of the dance," the voice had a hint of a smile to it. "And your screams echo through the jungle so nicely."

She stood up and stretched her back while she gazed out into the deep shadows of the jungle around her, a smile on her face. "Oh? Does teacher want to hear me scream again?"

A throaty chuckle answered her, then the soft rhythm of his drums. She turned to face him; he was a very large and handsome male from the village. Menzo was his name and he had promised her to help improve her dance for the coming of age festival. As he beat out the complex pattern on the bongos, she had to admire the way his arms rippled underneath his spotted coat. The white gloves he wore were strange; she had never seen those in the jungle before.

She started her dance. It called back to the hunt, beginning with slow, subtle movements to emulate the waiting, then the stalking of prey, followed by a frenzy of movement, the pounce, the struggle. The cycle would repeat until she was too exhausted to move. Menzo called out to her before she had made but two steps into the first phase.

"Stop, Stop!" Jacqueline froze and she looked at Menzo with a mortified expression. Had she screwed up already? She'd been practicing so hard. He shook his head sadly, clearly disappointed. "Your footing is all wrong. Let me show you." He tapped out a simpler version of the rhythm on his drums with those strange white gloves. Then with a quick motion, he pulled his hands from them and they kept drumming. Jacqueline blinked at that and her ears went back for a moment. Something about those gloves was wrong. They didn't belong in her jungle.

"Jacqueline, don't worry about those. Look at me."

The command peeled Jacqueline's eyes from the gloves to Menzo, and she couldn't help but be struck by how handsome he was, his wide chest sported a pattern of spots that perfectly accented his white tuxedo jacket. He took her paw in his and stepped behind her, pressing himself to her back and her paw in his to her stomach. As he did so, she got a nose full of his heady scent. Instinctively, she leaned up against him and was starting to curl her tail around his leg before she caught herself. She shook her head to clear it. She already had a mate and it wasn't Menzo. This was a practice, nothing more. "What am I doing wrong?"

"Jacqueline," his voice was a throaty purr that made her insides wibble, and her damn tail encircled his leg despite her attempts to stop it. "You have stand on your toes. Leopard Women have no heels, remember?" He slid his hands down her thighs. The touch sent bolts of warmth through her legs, and fur sprung forth and spread where his touch tickled her skin. The sensation made her push back against him, up on her toes as her breath shuddered. Her already strengthened legs thickened further as the fur flowed over them. First a downy white undercoat, followed by a thicker layer that mimicked the spotted coloration of her skin. Her feet lengthened, bursting out of the shoes she had completely forgotten about. The heels of her feet faded into her ankles as her toes sprouted wickedly curved claws. Menzo shifted his hands and began to tease the fur of her inner thighs, raking his claws through the thickening softness. Hot sexual need shot through Jacqueline. Growling, she reached back over her head and encircled his wide neck with her arms, pulling herself up to him to lick the underside of his muzzle.

As the front of her feet swelled into two massive paws, Menzo twisted away from her seeking tongue and clamped his jaws on the nape of her neck, Jacqueline cried out in pleasure he pulled her skin away from her bones. An impossible warmth spread from his fangs and into her toughing hide. Fur sprouted where his teeth made contact with her spotted skin, spreading around her neck and down over her breasts. She clenched her jaw and ground her teeth together as he changed his grip, biting her so hard that a lance of pain stabbed through the pleasure as one of his teeth pierced her hide and stabbed into her muscle. It drove the change deeper into her neck, stretching and thickening both muscle and bone. Powerful jaws can not help you if your prey can snap your neck.

Menzo pulled his teeth from Jacqueline's neck just as the fur crept up to her chin and there it halted for the moment. Jacqueline panted, her wide feline tongue protruding over the top of her black lower lip. Her face was the only part of her left unfurred, a humanish face mounted at the end of a thick animal neck, her brown hair, mane-like, cascading down its length. She could feel his breath on the fur on the back of her ears.

Waiting.

Her tongue flicked up over her nose and back into her mouth. The jungle had faded away; they were on the stage. Menzo was not a Leopard Man and she was on the cusp of losing all her humanity. Moistening her lips, she spoke two words, "Finish it."

Sliding his hands up her body, he cupped her breasts and teased her rock-hard nipples. She could only mrowl in encouragement, then yowl when the tease became a savage twist. "These just won't do, Jacqueline." A strange constriction gripped her chest, like a pulling sensation on the inside of her breasts. It was both uncomfortable and arousing, making her squirm in Menzo's grasp. His hands fell away and she grasped her breasts with her own paw-like hands. They felt odd to her, not quite the same heft as she remembered. Looking down to confirm it, after accounting for the thick covering of fur, her generous C-cup was now closer to a B-cup. "No!" She squeaked in horror; they were still shrinking! Her breasts had been the one thing she really liked about her body.

"Do not worry, my little huntress. What Leopard Women lack in size, they make up in abundance." As he spoke, he touched the spots directly below her now-smaller breasts and moved his fingers in a circular pattern. At first, Jacqueline didn't notice, entranced by the shrinking of her most prized feminine assets which seemed to settle on a modest B-cup, but as he continued, the flesh under the circles started to become quite sensitive.

Soon, Jacqueline panted with heat and didn't know why. The areas Menzo was stroking felt tight, like the skin there was being stretched. Craning her neck downward, she saw that there was no longer any fur under Menzo's fingers, instead an additional set of black nipples poked through her fur.

Then he pinched them.

Jacqueline roared as pleasure exploded from her new nubs. The roar faded into a moan as Menzo began to roll them against his thumb and forefingers. She writhed against him as they grew into breasts that were just a little smaller than the pair above.

Menzo seized them and sent Jacqueline's mind rocketing towards the stratosphere as she filled the room with an inhuman scream of bliss. "You know leopards have litters of three or four, sometimes five. How about an encore?" Without waiting for an answer, he pinched another twin patches of flesh. The fur immediately melted away from his fingers and two more nipples eagerly sprang into existence. When he grasped them, Jacqueline's own hands started to clutch at her top pair, squeezing them rhythmically as her body writhed. An indescribable pressure was building within her, something far more primal than the simple biological organism. As her third set of breasts swelled into their tiny existence, Jacqueline could feel herself on the precipice of something far more consequential.

"Yes. Just little bit more," whispered Menzo. He had let go of her fifth and sixth tits, each not much more than a nipple with a tiny bulge behind it, leaving her frozen, trembling on the edge of something massive. Now his fingers were inching downwards, sliding through the thick fur on her stomach towards the damp patch of fur between her legs. There was a sense of finality hanging between them; if she let him push her over this ledge, there would be no return.

She reached her paw toward his hand and stopped, hovering over it. There was no compulsion any more. To stop him, all she needed to do was push his hand away. That would mean going back

to what she was before. hat weak human with the pathetic job, and no magical talent whatsoever. Her body felt so wonderful like this, so right. She grabbed his hand and pushed it down towards her sex. His finger stroked across her lips once and Jacqueline mouth form an involuntary 'O' shape as she moaned in ecstasy. He touched her clit and Jacqueline felt something within begin to crack. Stroking it side to side sent spasms through her body, and she grabbed hold of the fey to prevent herself from falling down. "I-I-" but she couldn't finish the words as the bones of her face began to pop and distend. "Ahhhhh," was all she could manage as her face pushed out into a short muzzle, fur racing after her nose as long whiskers sprouted from her upper lip, the last of her human features consumed by her feral attributes.

Still the tension continued to build within her as Menzo continued to stroke her. Her body began to shake from the tension. Strangled growling sounds escaped her throat. Then, with a final press of his finger, the dam shattered. Jacqueline forced a scream of pleasure and triumph that nothing human could ever replicate. She felt something drop away from her, something she would never get back, but what did a leopardess need with humanity anyway?

Menzo held her as the aftershocks rocked her body. She slumped against him as her legs lost their strength. They stood there for a long moment. She felt the haze of pleasure, the magic starting to drain out of her, its work finished.

Done. She was done, but what was she now?

Opening her eyes, she saw the mirror that Menzo had bent her in front of earlier. The jungle and the bonfire of her dream were gone. She hung off a grinning, human-like Menzo, his impossible blue eyes shining. But it was her reflection that made her jaw drop. Huge amber eyes stared back at her, set in the face of an untamed animal, but with just enough humanity in it that you could see her smiling. Her coat glowed with health and her six breasts looked much bigger under the layer of fur that hid the nipples. The third set nearly invisible under her pelt-- hidden treasures. Her torso was long and gently curved. Thick, digitigrade legs gave her killer hips, and her nearly four-foot long tail loosely curled around Menzo leg.

"Do you admit to being a leopardess now, Jacqueline?"

"Yes." There was no hesitation in her deep, almost guttural voice. The word shivered through her, and she felt the magic within her bite into her very being, burrowing itself deep within her. Her form shimmered subtly; she could see the individual hairs that made up her pelt, and the texture of her eyes. Her body had just crossed the threshold from glamour to reality. There was no going back.

"Well, then. We'd best be going. Can't let the MDA find us," he flashed a grin and withdrew a small gold collar from his sleeve.

"No," Jacqueline answered, seemingly lost in her own reflection.

Menzo made to fasten the collar around her neck, but found he was unable to close the collar. Jacqueline had gotten her paw between her neck and the collar. His eyes widened. "Now, don't be silly. You need a sponsor to bring you to the fey wilds."

"You are not my mate," she growled. Her mind was confused, where was the jungle? Where was Dave? She knew instinctively that a collar was something she did not want. She focused on that, raising another paw to entangle the collar.

"Jacqueline, lower your paw."

The paw trembled but did not move.

They stared at each other for a moment through the mirror. Her with a stubborn, just slightly teeth bared, expression; his of disbelief that was rapidly changing to anger.

The silence was shattered by the echoing "BANG!" of the night-club door flying open. Both Jacqueline and Menzo started.

"FREEZE! MDA!"

The Magical Defense Agency had arrived. Finally.

CHAPTER 2

BREAKING THE NEWS

DR. NIDDLER STRAIGHTENED THE AMULET AROUND HIS NECK AND smoothed his lab coat in front of the large cold iron door that opened into the waiting room in the hospital's magical injury ward. "This never gets any easier," he muttered to himself. Sighing, he punched the big red button next to the door and it wheeled aside with a metallic creak. Dr. Niddler looked out into the waiting room, double-checked the name on his clipboard and called, "Mr. David Hopla." A very weary looking man stood up from a chair and hurried over.

"How is she? What happened to her? They haven't told me anything. It's been two days!" The questions came rapid-fire, full of frantic worry. The doctor did not answer immediately and only uttered a long sigh before stepping aside and gesturing for Dave to enter the ward. Only once he was in and the door rolled closed, did Dr. Niddler speak.

"They didn't tell you anything?"

Dave shook his head, "Nothing. The MDA called my cell and told me that Jacqueline was involved in a magical incident and was here for treatment. Please, is she okay?"

Dr. Niddler frowned. "I'm afraid 'okay' isn't a word I would use to describe your wife's case, Mr. Hopla. Your wife attracted the attention of a fey noble in the midst of a hunt for mortal acquisitions. Somehow, she held him off long enough for the MDA to get a lock on him. Your wife must have had an iron will and was very happy with you to last that long."

Dave put his hand over his mouth. "Have had?" His eyes widened with fear.

Sighing, the doctor started walking down the hallway, gesturing Dave to follow. "Well, maybe she still does. She's never been here before, so we're not sure how much of her original personality is intact." He stopped when he felt Dave's hand on his shoulder.

"Please, doctor. Stop dancing around and tell me what's wrong with her. Is anything left?"

The doctor bowed his head. "Sorry. I'm not very good at this. I should have requested a councilor be present." He steadied himself and looked Dave in the eye. "Mr. Hopla, your wife has been afflicted by a recursive glamour."

"A what?"

"Do you understand glamour at all?"

"Yeah, it's fey magic. Illusions. Don't they disappear with the fey?"

"Almost correct. They are illusions that are as real as the afflicted believe they are, and they do generally fade in a short time without the presence of a fey to maintain them. However, this utter bastard used glamour to dominate an entire audience and used their belief to rewrite Mrs. Hopla."

"What?"

"He attempted to reshape your wife's body and mind into that of a pet and he partially succeeded."

"But… But it's glamour. It wasn't real, right?"

Dr. Niddler bit back another sigh. "Technically, it was not. But with all the force of 200 people fueling the glamour, the fey was able to convince your wife that she was as the glamour presented her. Once he did that, it created a feedback loop of belief. That's the theory."

"I don't understand."

The doctor frowned and tried again. "The fey cast a glamour on your wife that made it appear that she was inhuman, and she was then convinced to embrace the glamour as her actual identity. Now her own belief is feeding the glamour. We think he actually bent her soul to fuel it. It has resisted every single attempt to dispel it, and each attempt causes her so much pain, I am reluctant to make more attempts."

"Pain?"

The little doctor nodded. "I've never seen anything like it. It's almost as if she has become part fey herself. Cold iron makes her very uncomfortable and its touch burns. Not nearly as much as it would a true fey creature, but it burns all the same. Magic just flows over her as if she was born this way. I'm sorry, but besides a mental evaluation to ensure she's not a danger to the public, there isn't much more we can do for her other than offer you both therapy sessions to help you adjust to her new body."

Dave just blinked, "What is she?"

"I can't tell you that. It would reinforce the glamour."

"But you said she's stuck anyway!"

"I know, but it's hospital policy on glamours-- no preconceptions allowed. She's behind that door. Number 10." He pointed down the hall.

Dave looked at the door and back at the doctor.

"Passcode is 321. Just enter it and turn the handle."

With a sigh, he went over to the door and punched in the code, turned the handle and opened the door. His eyes widened as he looked within, "Jacqueline?"

"Dave?" The voice was low and husky. Then a mass of gold and black sprung from the room and into Dave, nearly knocking him to the floor. The leopardess wrapped arms, legs and tail around him in a desperate embrace. Dave staggered backwards until he reached the wall to take the rest of the load. "Oh god, I thought they were never going to let you come in! They tried to take my spots away! They said I'm sick! I want to go home!" The words came rushing out in a voice that was not his wife's, but the way she said that all in a rush was 100% unhappy Jacqueline.

Dave looked down the back of this creature that had been, or still was, his wife. He looked helplessly at Dr. Niddler. The doctor mimed a hug, and then a petting motion. Dave closed his eyes and slowly returned the embrace, his hands shaking as he did so. Her fur was soft and warm as his fingers slipped through it. "It's okay, Jacq. I'm here now."

This was going to take some getting used to.

CHAPTER 3

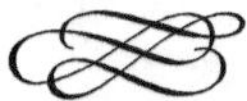

THE MAN FROM THE MDA

"Alright, Mr. Hopla. These are the guardianship, release and magical damage insurance forms. You should read and initial each page." The stooge from the Magical Defense Agency dropped a nearly two inch stack of paper on the table between him and Dave. The man would have been a unmemorable civil servant if not for the jagged scar that went across his nose and followed his cheek bone all the way to his ear. He placed a large worn hand on top of the pile of papers and gave Dave a hard look with his steel grey eyes. "Although, if you're smart, you'll walk out that door and start making divorce arrangements."

Dave's eyes, previously nearly closed from the long day of forms and paperwork he had already filled out, snapped open. His feet hit the floor like two hammers as he stood up with enough force that his chair was sent sprawling backwards, clattering against the tile floor. "What did you say?"

The MDA agent didn't even blink. "Just stating my professional opinion, Mr. Hopla. I have seen this before and it never ends well."

Dave glared at the man. "I've heard quite enough from Doctor Christof about how it will end. I've been warned all about her jaw strength and how we should just put her down."

"Doctors Christof and Niddler have been playing good doctor and bad doctor for a very long time, Mr. Hopla. Usually, they both make good points. Your wife is gone, Mr. Hopla. That creature is harmed by iron."

"So are MDA wizards!"

"Not the point. She's no longer human. She's a magical creature and that means that magic is going to wrap itself around everything close to her, including you, your family and your neighbors. Normal will not exist; and that's only if those two bullets managed to knock some sense into the Fey that attacked her. Which, in my professional opinion, I doubt."

"I will take that under advisement." Dave's fists were balled and he could feel his nails start to break the skin of his palms.

The man simply shrugged and pushed the packet of papers across the table. "Right. Well, when you're done with these take them to reception. The terms are standard and non-negotiable. You may want to have a lawyer look them over, but the crux of it is simple. You assume legal responsibility for Mrs. Jacqueline Hopla's actions unless the government certifies her as a moral actor." He then stood, eyes betraying nothing but indifference to Dave's baleful glare. "Have as pleasant as possible day."

After the grey-eyed man departed, Dave grimaced and shook his head. He wondered if all MDA agents were that bitter. Sighing, he skimmed the dense legalese on the top piece of paper. Due to cost, a lawyer was going to be out of the question, they'd barely be able to pay for Jacqueline's two week stay in the hospital.

He was going to need coffee, lots of coffee.

CHAPTER 4

THERAPY

"NO!"

Dr. Niddler ducked as black keys rocketed across the room, launched by the impact of Jacqueline's paws crashing down on the innocent keyboard. She dug her claws into its plastic casing and snapped it in half with an ear splitting CRACK! Throwing the pieces down onto the floor below her, Jacqueline rounded on the Doctor, baring her bright whites fangs and growling. "This is not my keyboard! You're trying to trick me!"

The doctor stood up and flicked off a small shard of plastic that had landed on the front of his lab coat. Then he gave Jacqueline a tiny smile. "It is, well, was, the same keyboard you have been using for years, Mrs. Hopla."

"That's impossible!" Jacqueline shifted her gaze down at her thick fingers and flexed them experimentally, causing a wicked claw to extend from each digit. One of the claws had snapped on the black plastic and she winced as she felt the pain welling up from it a bit belatedly. There was no way her paw-like hands could use a human keyboard in any sort of comfort. It had been awkward when she tried, the pads of her fingers were wider than the keys themselves.

The keyboard had looked awfully familiar, but it couldn't have been hers. She had been born as a Leopard Woman, from the jungles of South America, there was no way she could have obtained her typing speed of one hundred words per minute on the equipment she had just shattered.

Slowly, Doctor Niddler crossed the room and put his hand over the soft spotted fur of her hand paw.

Jacqueline looked up at him, feeling tears welling up in her eyes, anticipating what came next. "Please. This, this isn't my keyboard. I must have had a special one, built for my hands." It sounded good to her, that must have been how it happened. Still, as she finished the explanation her ears folded against her head in an effort to mute the words she knew were coming.

"Consider another possibility for me Jacqueline. Perhaps these..." He gave the paw a gentle squeeze, "are not the hands you used to type on this keyboard."

She snatched her paw again from him, cradling it to her chest. "No..." She whispered but it was too late. In her mind's eye she was sitting at her desk, listening to the clicking clatter of the keyboard filling the air as her fingers danced over it. No claws to get in the way, no pads that hit the wrong keys, just long, graceful fingers finding their places with the sureness of decades of practice. She mewled, protesting against the sudden flash of memory and turned herself away from the doctor, trying to hide her paws from his grey eyes. Eyes that wanted her to be something she wasn't.

"Jacqueline," Dr. Niddle's voice was both gentle and insistent. No matter how loudly she growled or roared at him he stayed infuriatingly clam, radiating that subtle depression that he always seemed to wallow in. She felt his hand press against the fur on her back. "Please imagine having those hands again. Wouldn't it be better? You could use the keyboards, surf the Internet, go back to work."

She hissed. "No! Those are not my hands. Not now!" Every day had been the same. For the past two weeks, Doctor Niddler would come in to her room and poke holes in her memories. It was as if there were two Jacqueline's in her head and they had been jumbled together in a cement mixer. The Doctor was slowly separating the pieces of her into separate piles. He'd give her objects she remembered using but found to her horror that they were incompatible with her body. It had been terrifying to learn that her memories were not trustworthy. She had been very cooperative initially, but now, after two weeks in this little room getting poked, prodded and occasionally tortured by the sadistic Doctor Christhof, she didn't give a damn anymore. Maybe she really had been human once. So what? She wasn't human now and didn't want to be. She just wanted to go home. It didn't matter to her whether home was in apartment or in a jungle-- as long as it was with Dave, she'd manage. It had to be better than just seeing him for an hour a day.

"Come now. Lets try that visualization technique we were doing yesterday. Imagine past the spots."

"NO!" Jacqueline sprung from the chair she was sitting on and into her bed, where she curled herself in the tightest ball her spine would allow. "I don't care! I'm done. Go away."

There was a pause, then the doctor sighed deeply. Jacqueline flinched, she always felt he was disappointed in her when he did that. "Very well. I will see you tomorrow, Mrs. Hopla."

Jacqueline did not budge until she heard the buzzing click of the door locking behind him. Even then she only uncurled her spotted body enough so she could find a comfortable sleeping position.

CHAPTER 5

THE FAINT SOUND OF A VOICE DRIFTING INTO JACQUELINE'S EARS WAS enough to rouse her from her fitful slumber, it was the one voice she pined to hear, Dave's voice. Her ears zeroed in on the sound as her large amber eyes opened. The tip of her tail twitched with anticipation as she strained to make out the words.

"...Signed all the papers." He was down the hall somewhere. She counted two more sets of foot falls, hard shoes, doctor shoes. They were all getting closer.

"Mark my words, Mr. Hopla, you are making a mistake!" Jacqueline's lips curled up into a sneer when she recognized the whiny tones of Dr. Christhof. The sadist that seemed to believe that curing her was a distant second to keeping her alive. "She's dangerous! Far too unstable to be released!"

Another voice, Dr. Niddler, "Poking a sleeping person with an iron rod tends to produce a negative response Christhof."

Christhof sniffed, "I had to administer the iron sensitivity test." Jacqueline felt her hackles rise, the little bastard had woken her up from a nap by prodding her ass with a six foot long crowbar. It felt as if she'd been poked with a hot iron. Confused and in pain she had attacked him, managing to nick him with her claws before an orderly had gotten a riot shield between her and the doctor.

"Well, I was certainly not getting close to her! Do you have any idea how strong she is?" Christhof whined.

The footsteps stopped dead and silence filled the air, followed by the soft clicking of teeth grinding together, Dave only did that when he was extremely angry.

A sigh filled the air. "We need to work on your bedside manner, Dr. Christhof."

"And you wonder why I want to take her home?" Dave's voice broke in.

"Home." The word slipped out from Jacqueline's lips in disbelief. Dave was trying to get her out of here! Relief flooded her at the mere possibility of leaving this place and its antiseptic stench. She had an urge to break the door down and roar "FREEDOM!" into the hallway. However, she knew the door would withstand the assault, its wood bore the scars. Instead she slipped off her bed and assumed a crouching position in front of the door, preparing to jump Dave when he opened it. Her long spotted tail lashed behind her with such speed and excitement that you might say it was wagging.

Jacqueline strained to hear the conversation. "I don't blame you for wanting to take her, Mr. Hopla, but I wish you'd give me a bit more time. Another two weeks at least, we're making some progress with the confrontation therapy and it will be less effective if she's in a familiar environment."

"I still don't understand why you are wasting time with that therapy." Christhof cut in. "She's too far gone. You'll never undo that physical transformation by talking the magic out of her. A magic siphon is a far simpler approach."

"How many times must I tell you not to even mention that medieval practice! I am never going to allow you to strap a patient to a slab of iron! That isn't treatment! It's torture!" Dr. Niddler's voice was clipped.

"But it works!" Dr. Christhof protested.

There was a whap of flesh on flesh.

"I suggest you leave now, Christhof. I am going to have a very long talk with the directors already, but if you don't, I will happily release Mr. Hopla's fist."

Jacqueline grinned at the receding sound of footsteps, then deepened her crouch, setting up her legs to propel her through the door. Silently she urged them to stop talking and just open the damn thing.

"My apologies, Mr. Hopla. Dr. Christhof is a very good doctor for cases he believes he can cure. Over the years he has gotten… intolerant of cases he cannot 'fix.'"

"He is not helping your case for keeping her here."

"Indeed."

The heavy footsteps of Dr. Niddler's shoes resumed their progress toward her room, Dave must have been wearing sneakers since Jacqueline couldn't track him at all. Her body tensed as the sounds stopped in front of her door, the tip of her tail twitched with excitement.

The buzz of the lock announced a visitor and Jacqueline launched herself towards the door as it opened without seeing who had opened it. There was a cry of surprise as she felt her arms close around someone who was a bit skinny for Dave.

She quickly released doctor Niddler as she felt her ears start to burn with embarrassment. "Sorry, Doctor."

"Quite alright, Jacqueline," he chuckled as he straightened his lab coat. "It would appear that the sound proofing on your room isn't what I was led to believe."

"Over here Jacq." Now THAT was Dave's voice-- deep, rich and just a hint of a geeky squeak to it. He was tall to her, just under six feet, dressed in smart looking khakis and a black, button down shirt. The smart business casual look was then ruined by the ancient, brown leather jacket he wore over it; she loved the dusky scent of it. Just seeing him was usually enough to melt her depression, and now with prospect of actually leaving this place, it was sending her mind racing with all the things she wanted to do to him once they actually had some privacy. Growling excitedly, she momentarily fell to all fours to circle around his body, rubbing the side of her muzzle against his clothing, drinking in his scent while marking him with her own. "Jacq?" his voice had just a pinch of unease to it.

She chuffed in amusement as she circled around him again, letting the growl fade into a rumbling purr. Dave always got a little nervous when she let the cat side show, but she didn't care right now. Pushing herself off her handpaws, she coiled up around his body like a snake climbing a tree, making sure to press every curve of her body against him. She heard his breath catch as she slipped a spotted arm under his jacket, pressing herself against his chest so he could feel all six of her breasts as she slid them up his torso to meet his lips with her muzzle. Her free hand circled around to the back of his neck, giving her additional leverage as they shared a deep kiss.

Meeting his lips to her muzzle had been a very strange experience at first. Their lips were sized differently and interlocked a bit oddly. When she was in a pondering mood, the fact that they didn't know how to kiss each other after 4 years of marriage was a point for Dr. Niddler's supposition that her memories had been mucked with. But they were definitely getting better at it now, as their tongues flirted with each other.

Only after Dr. Niddler coughed once did Jacqueline and Dave's lips part. Dave gave a little shudder as he did so, a telltale sign that, human or not, Jacqueline still had the proper effect on her husband. She looked deep into his dark brown eyes; there was uncertainty there along with a good helping of the worried bags under his eyes. "Is it true? We can go home?"

He smiled then, "Yeah, Jacqueline. We're going home. I signed all the paperwork this morning." Jacqueline chuffed again and hugged Dave until she heard his spine pop.

"Oops, sorry."

"Its okay, Jacq." Dave's voice sounded a little weak.

CHAPTER 6

ADJUSTMENTS

Uncertainty gnawed at Dave as he sat in Dr. Niddler's office, watching the man deftly fill out the mountain of release paperwork while Dave held his wife's… paw. He could feel the rough texture of her pad on his palm, the softness of the fur under his fingers, but strangest of all was the sheer size of it. Her paw was so wide that he could barely curl his fingers around it. Just two week ago his hand would have completely engulfed hers. Her grip tightened on his hand and Dave turned to look at her.

Jacqueline was watching the doctor with an almost feral intensity as he continued to sign and initial documents with a machine like efficiency. Dave swallowed and took a good look at what his wife had become, the creature he would be sleeping next to tonight. What a beautiful creature she was, too. Her spotted fur rippled over her muscular curves and she moved with an inhuman grace that oozed power and femininity. Just watching her elevated Dave's heartbeat, and stirred a primal feeling deep inside him, urging him to take hold of her and not let go. He tried to focus on those feelings and ignore the bubbles of doubt that kept rising within him. On the edge of taking her home, Dave struggled to keep a lid on the part of himself that was repulsed by those same inhuman features.

The voice of the MDA man from the day before echoed through his head as Dave's eyes roamed Jacqueline's body. They followed the strange curves of her crossed digitigrade legs up, under the fabric of her skirt and down the length of her tail, the tip of it curling and then straightening on the floor. A little voice in his head screamed at the top of its intangible lungs that she wasn't remotely human, that she was a freakish beast. It cited all the things that disturbed him: the second pair of mounds on her long torso that strained against the now too small shirt he had brought her and, most of all, her face. Her hair, a mane of curly brown hair, framed the facial features of leopard but with black, human-like lips at the end of the muzzle and golden eyes that glittered with intelligence. Taken together, Dave registered a degree of wrongness looking at her face. A mask that was too realistic; a cartoon from a Disney film made uncannily real. Nobody would recognize her as Jacqueline Hopla.

And yet, she was definitely Jacqueline. Her voice was different, lower, hovering just above a growl as she spoke, yet the flow of her voice was the same as it always had been. If he closed his eyes and listened to her, Dave could imagine her as her old self. Her humor, her wit, her streak of naughtiness were all intact. Even the depression she had fallen into the past week was something Dave recognized. She had always hated being cooped up. That was pure Jacqueline, not the cat.

Dave gave her paw-like hand, or perhaps hand-like paw, a squeeze and those amber eyes turned to face him. Her expression was not easy to read, there was a small quirk on the left side of her muzzle, and her tail began to move with strong, full length lashes behind her. Excitement? Not quite. Her eyes blinked slowly and her black lips moved silently, mouthing three words, "I love you." The grip on Dave's hand tightened and relaxed. He felt his own lips break into a smile as he squeezed back, a calming sensation moving through him. He did love this woman, and she loved him back, that would have to be enough for now. He pushed the part of him that was terrified that the changes would get in the way of that love to the back of mind.

There was a click as Dr. Niddler set his pen down on the desk and spoke, pulling Dave from his thoughts. "There we are," he said, as if the words themselves were part of a sigh. He took a small portion of the papers, folded them into thirds, then placed them into an envelope and handed it to Jacqueline. "These are your temporary identification papers, it is important to keep them with you at all times. The MDA will send you a permanent one in a few weeks. It will come with a collar but you can put the charm on anything you wish."

Dave watched Jacqueline's ears droop slightly as she took the papers, he understood why. The government did not generally recognize magical non-humans as legal persons until they had gone through an intensive evaluation that would certify them to be free of any sort of behaviors that would harm human beings. Jacqueline, as a dedicated carnivore with a clear hunting instincts might never pass it. Until then, Dave was her legal guardian and she would be considered either an indebted servant or a pet. They had talked about it and had agreed this was preferable to staying in the hospital for years, but Dave knew it chafed her pride.

The doctor gave Dave the remaining pile of papers, which he dutifully placed in a folder, then slipped into a waiting spot in his attaché case. Dave zipped it closed and looked up at the doctor, "Anything else?"

He breathed one of those heavy sighs that Dave was getting used to. The doctor lived under a heavy burden and made that clear to everyone who met him. "Not unless you're willing to give us another two weeks."

"I think this will be better in the long run, Doctor."

"I'll be better off at home," Jacqueline chimed in.

He smiled at her. "Could I talk to you in private for a moment, Jacqueline? Just for a few minutes."

She blinked and her ears turned backwards for a split second before facing forward again. "Uh, sure." Dave felt her paw tighten on his hand as she leaned over and gave his cheek a brief lick. The rough tongue felt harsh on the stubble of his cheek. "Give us a minute hon. I'll be right out."

"Alright, I'll wait outside." The lick/kiss was another thing that was off-putting. He could feel the affection behind it, but that tongue of hers hurt. Especially if she did it twice on the same spot. He gave her handpaw another gentle squeeze, then rose to his feet and exited the room, shutting the door behind him.

Dave was left standing outside with only his lingering doubts for company. Out of Jacqueline's presence, they crept out from the shadows of his mind. He wondered for umpteenth time if this really was the best thing for Jacqueline. He had been so confident yesterday as he went through that pile of paperwork. Now, he had a fresh reminder of all the little ways she was and wasn't the woman he married. Dr. Niddler had told him from day one not to hope for a total reversion, but had said that the confrontation therapy had been known to cause physical adjustments in recursive glamour patients that would allow their remembered lives to be possible. Small things like hand shapes, posture and facial expressions might shift with time-- the magic might have gone so deep to alter her soul as well as her flesh. So far, Jacqueline's therapy had not affected her form one iota, and she still insisted she had been a leopard for her entire life.

The source of the trouble, according to Dr. Christhof, was that Jacqueline had no desire to be human. A hypothesis that even made Dr. Niddler nod sadly when Dave admitted to them that Jacqueline had always been interested in magic and the Fey in particular. The infection didn't have to invade, she could have invited it in, they said. That was preposterous, though. If she had accepted the magic, she'd be curled up at the foot of some twiggy-looking Fey at the moment.

If he could just snap her out of her delusions. Maybe, just maybe, he'd have his Jacqueline back. All Dave could do was hope.

Dave was so lost in his thoughts that he did not hear the door creak open behind him. He started as two spotted arms threaded under his own and encircled his chest. Around the left wrist was something new, a plain sliver bracelet with a black stone set in the center of it. He shivered as whiskers tickled the side of his neck, followed by the soft fuzz of her muzzle as Jacqueline pressed herself against his back. He forced himself to relax and leaned back against her. Reaching up, he spread his fingers and threaded them through the fur of her arm and curled his fingers around her elbow. It was a soft, inviting texture with a trace of coarseness that seemed to evaporate if you pressed against it. You could feel the individual strands of hair and see a few of them float off into the air. There was nothing illusory about them.

She squeezed him tight, and neither said anything for a moment. Dave let his worries seep away in her arms.

Eventually, Dave stirred and poked at the bracelet. "Should I be jealous?"

She snorted and then chuckled, it was more a hurr hurr than a ha ha. "Nah, Dr. Niddler probably has a drawer full of them. He's a good guy when it's not a therapy session."

"Are you coming back for therapy?"

"Uh…" She squeezed him a little tighter and Dave thought he might have heard a little growl. "No?"

"Jacq…" She had him immobilized for the moment so he just turned his head and attempted to give her a stern look from the corner of his eyes. She sighed. "Dr. Niddler gave me a list of therapists, but wants to see me here once a week. I don't… Can we just go home?"

Dave turned and kissed her on the nose, "Oh god, yes."

CHAPTER 7

HOMECOMING

Jacqueline caught more than a whiff of fear on Dave as they walked out of the hospital's magical ward. It didn't take long to figure out the source of his apprehension. Once out of the ward, people would freeze as she entered their vision. It didn't seem to matter who they were or what they were doing. One man poured his coffee down his shirt as his head swiveled away from his drink in order to track her down the hallway. Some recovered soon after the freeze, turning away from her uncomfortably, but most stared at her until something got between her and their vision. Jacqueline found herself touching her front to make sure the blouse she put on had not mysteriously vanished. She was even wearing a skirt despite the uncomfortable way it pressed her tail between her buttocks. Was it her additional sets of breasts maybe? The blouse hung a bit oddly on her torso but Jacqueline had hoped the lower sets were too small to arouse a human's interest.

Surely they had seen her kind before? She didn't remember getting so many stares before her accident. It unnerved her. She struggled to keep her claws sheathed and her fangs behind her lips, channeling her nervous energy into her tail, which lashed behind her like an animated whip. She and Dave walked through the corridors, hand in paw, toward the parking garage, keeping her head up and refusing to make eye contact. She had been out of the jungle for a decade, she should be used to this. So should Dave.

They reached the car, climbed in and both sighed with relief. After taking a moment to adjust her tail so she wasn't putting too much weight on it, they were on their way. Dave prattled a bit about how he'd gotten lots of concerned calls from her friends that she had been out with the night of the accident. One of them kept dropping off food. Jacqueline mostly just nodded during the two-hour drive. There were plenty of things she wanted to do once she got home, but nothing that required discussion. Instead she watched the scenery of the city fall away as they made their way towards their little burb. The scenery was familiar, but it made her brain itch uncomfortably.

The Accident, she couldn't quite recall it. She had been in a theater and had met someone? It was all just a grey blur after that. The accident had something to do with everyone's strange insistence that she had been human once, a fey attack or something... What nonsense, she remembered growing up in the Connecticut jungle tree village, her father had been a lawyer, her mother was a traditionalist and did all the hunting and cooking... Jacqueline's train of thought derailed. Mother hated blood; fainted at sight of it. How could she hunt? Dad must have done the hunting... must have. She shifted her attention back to Dave. He was much easier to focus on than thinking of her family. Memories didn't matter really. The future was ahead of them and all she had seen of him in the past two weeks was an hour a day. Planning out what she was going to do to him once they got home in exacting detail was far more fun than glooming over the past.

However, those pleasurable thoughts couldn't block the sense of dread that crept over her when Dave pulled the car into the parking lot of an apartment building. "Home sweet home!" He announced with a happy grin, which froze on his face when he saw that Jacqueline's ears were pressed flat against her head. "What's wrong?

Jacqueline licked her nose in a nervous gesture. "This is home?"

"I-I thought we had a house... on the edge of the woods." No

leopard would ever willingly confine themselves to just an apartment. She needed to hunt and claim a small territory to sate the
jungle born instincts. Urban living was almost as bad as being in
a zoo.

Dave petted her leg and gave her a sad smile. "That was our first
house, a rental, we moved into town to cut down on the commute.
Remember?"

That last word hit her like an ice pick. A sharp pain stabbed
through the front of her brain forcing her eyes closed as her face
twisted into a snarl. Her body shook as that lance of pain began to
twist. Memories flashed through her, too quick to be seen, as something deep within her shifted. Jacqueline let out a strangled hiss as
the pain vanished and she slumped against the door of the car.

"Jacqueline?" Dave reached over and grabbed her shoulder, eyes
wide with fear and concern.

Jacqueline had to wait a moment to catch her breath. "I'm
okay," she said with what she hoped was a smile.

"Maybe the doc was right. We should go back."

"NO!" The word ripped out of Jacqueline like a roar, loud
enough to echo in the confines of the car. Dave flinched away from
her, slamming his back against his door. They both blinked at each
other, Jacqueline feeling about as shocked as he looked. She
lowered her eyes and hugged herself. "Sorry. Just give me a minute
okay? I think I remember now." That was the truth. That pain,
whatever it was, seemed to have loosened some bits in her brain.
She remembered the apartment and moving into it. Somehow, it
had been her idea. It didn't make any sense to her, but the memory
was there. How had she lived in a 3rd floor apartment for two years
without driving herself insane? Could the stress of it be related to
her accident? There was nothing she could do about it now. She
ran her claws through her head fur to pull it out of her eyes and
sighed.

Dave exhaled, "You sure that you are okay?"

Jacqueline gave the back of her paw a few comfort licks before
answering, "Yeah, I'm okay." She remembered what Dr. Niddler
had said right before they left. The world remembered her as a

human, no matter what the actual reality was. Dave included. It had slipped her mind. Why was that so hard to remember?

Steeling herself, she checked the parking lot for gawkers as she fumbled at the door handle. Seeing that the parking lot was mostly empty she popped the door open and stepped into the city air, away from the scent of Dave's fear. She forced a toothy grin onto her muzzle and pushed her ears forward, but was unable to stop the tip of her tail from curling with her nervousness. She clutched at her purse, her claws driving through the soft, black leather. Several heartbeats later, Dave climbed out of the car and circled around to her. Cautiously, he threaded his hands around her waist, drawing her into a tight embrace. "Come on, Jacq," he whispered and kissed her between her ears. She rumbled appreciatively at him, his touch was comforting. Taking her by the paw, he led her into the building.

With each step, the sense of familiarity grew and by the time they had reached the staircase, Jacqueline was certain she had walked this path hundreds of times before. Yet something was off about it. There was a chemical scent in the hallways. The three flights of stairs seemed to be spaced a little differently, tripping her up, a clawed toe snaring the carpet at one point. At the top of the stairs, they came to a nondescript door-- their door-- apartment 42. Dave unlocked it with a nervous flourish.

He looked back at Jacqueline to flash her an impish grin, although she could still see the worry in his eyes. Then, he turned the knob and threw the door open to reveal a living room festooned with yellow and black balloons with a big banner that read, "WEL-COME HOME," in large, cheery letters.

Jacqueline's jaw dropped, Dave chuckled as he pulled her into the room and closed the door behind them. "Well, the doctors nixed meeting many people on your first night home, but I had already bought all these balloons…"

"So you thought a party for two." Jacqueline gave a little growl, hopped forward and planted an aggressive kiss on his lips. "Just like our first date," she said after pulling back a micrometer. They had met at a disastrous surprise party, nearly ten years before. It had been for a mutual friend. Jacqueline had come early to help set up and a freak storm had turned the roads to ice while they were there. Nobody else had showed up and they were stranded in Dave's apartment for nearly two days. They had fallen fast for each other in that apartment.

"Maaaybe." He grinned briefly before Jacqueline attacked him with another kiss. This time she pushed back his lips, allowing her rough tongue to briefly flirt with his slick one. She would have pressed deeper but he pulled away, breaking the kiss, leaving Jacqueline aching for more.

"Would my kitten like to start this date with dinner?"

Jacqueline's tongue traced the outline of her muzzle, "That depends on what it is and how long it takes to cook. I may decide to skip to dessert." A single claw ran down the front of Dave's shirt, weaving in and out of the line of buttons down the front.

"Well, if you want to skip a slow-baked, orange honey-glazed ham, be my guest. It's all ready right now.

"Now?" Jacqueline's eyes widened, "but that takes hours!" It had been one of her favorite meals before she had declared herself a vegetarian.

"I know, it took me all morning to get it right." He took her hand and led her into the kitchen. There on the dining room table was a meat lover's feast for two. The promised ham, along with two small steaks and topped off with a side of bacon. The ham looked great, shining with the sugary glaze with an entire orange's worth of slices spiraled over the thick slice of ham.

"Oh, Dave…" Jacqueline fletched, forcing the air up into the roof of her mouth, expecting to taste the mouth-watering scents of the food before her. Nothing. That was strange. Another look at the food and she noticed that the steam rising from the food wasn't rising at all, it was actually frozen in the air. "Oh my god, Dave. Is that a stasis charm?"

"Yep. Sadly, this one is single use. Called in a favor at work. Ready to eat?" He stepped forward and smudged a circle drawn around the table. The steam instantly resumed rising from the food.

Closing her eyes Jacqueline breathed in, expecting to take in the warm, meaty scents of the food but was instead treated to a spike of pain. On top of all that wonderfulness, a sharp scent threaded between her nostrils like rusty barbed wire, burning her with its acidic harshness. Crying out in pain, she clapped her hands over her nose in a futile effort to block out the smell. Her mind reeled as it tried to place the awful scent and she fought to keep her stomach from adding its contents to the mix. The acid…citrus. The orange! But she loved citrus fruit! She used to swipe lemons from her mother when she cooked and eat them straight.

Pain! The pain of that scent seized her head like a vise and squeezed down on her. A whimper escaped her and she sank to her knees as pieces her of mind seemed to grind together like improperly sized gears. No, she never liked citrus fruit! It was an awful, evil scent; no self-respecting cat would ever tolerate the things. And she, Jacqueline, was born a cat and would die a cat. Dave had to have known this after four years of living with her! How stupid could the man be!

Dave chose that time to kneel down and touch her shoulder. "Jacq? What's wrong?"

An inhuman snarl tore from her as she spun around, snapping her jaws at Dave's arm. He jerked back just in time to avoid her teeth. Jacqueline didn't care; the hot sting of betrayal tinged her vision with red as she growled at her husband. She leaped at him, her large paws ramming into his chest and driving him into the floor. He screamed something but Jacqueline didn't hear it. His hands clutched at her fur for a brief moment before she caught his wrists. Snarling, she slammed them into the hardwood floor, pinning him under her. A roar unleashed directly in his face reduced his desperate struggles to quivering. "You ruined it! Why? You poisoned all that wonderful MEAT!" Her voice was intermixed with an angry growl.

"But… It's your favorite." Dave managed to whisper through lips white from terror.

She snarled at him. Dave whimpered in fear. "I never liked that! Never! That is something humans eat! I am NOT human! NEVER will be! When will you learn that!" For emphasis she let go of his wrists and used her claws to rip deep grooves in the hardwood floor

on either side of his head. Then she snorted, glared down at him with angry amber eyes and got off of him. Her tail brushed his face as she turned and stalked off towards the bedroom on all fours. The entire apartment shook from the force she used to slam the door closed.

CHAPTER 8

A GIFT AND A DANCE

IT WAS SEVERAL MINUTES BEFORE DAVE TRUSTED HIMSELF TO MOVE from where Jacqueline had left him. He forced his trembling limbs to push himself into the kitchen corner. He hugged his knees and let his head fall between them. Each shuddering breath threatening to transmute into a sob. Niddler had been right; taking her home had been stupid. He closed his eyes, but found Jacqueline's flashing white fangs waiting for him in the darkness behind his eyelids. The doctor had said that Jacqueline could be aggressive when her beliefs in the past were directly challenged, but he had brushed the warning off, foolishly trusting that his half a foot of height advantage would be enough. How wrong he had been.

Dave's gaze shifted to the deep grooves Jacqueline's claws had torn in the floor and shuddered anew. Jacqueline's raw speed and strength had caught him by surprise. There had been no chance for him to resist, no chance at all. He unconsciously rubbed his throat, his mind's eye seeing those teeth clamping around it, then watching her spots blur together as she tore it from his neck. If that had been her goal, there would have been absolutely nothing Dave could have done to stop her.

If they did fix this-- if they managed to work through her faulty memories and find stability-- Dave realized now that he was the delicate flower of the pair. There was a part him that questioned if he could even handle that. There were thousands of little ways that being bigger and stronger than her defined their relationship. From forcing a needed hug on her when she was grumpy, to tickling her when he lost an argument, to the way they made love. It would all be different now.

A scream of rage from the bedroom sliced through Dave's morose pondering. A bang echoed down the hallway, followed by a serial clicking. He groaned and let his head fall back into the cabinet behind him, he had a good idea what Jacqueline had just gotten into. The sound of tearing fabric combined with another inhuman roar confirmed it. Her wardrobe, her human wardrobe, was still in her closet with all those memories waiting to fly in the face of her belief that she had been born as she was now. Dave felt sick. That was another thing he should have gotten rid of for now, along with all the photos. Now all of her clothes would be ruined.

The ripping and shredding noises from the bedroom continued, occasionally punctuated by a growl or snarl. Dave sat and listened. They were getting slower as time went on. He closed his eyes and took a deep breath, an image of Jacq as the Tasmanian Devil whirling around their bedroom played through his imagination and he half-snorted. It was almost funny.

Slowly, Dave got to his feet. He went over to the corner of the room where a large box sat, black with a large leopard print ribbon tied around it. He lifted off the top. Inside lay a thick photo album. He opened it; on the first page was a large print of Jacqueline, her human smile beamed up at him. Dave put a hand on the photo for a moment and then closed the book with a frown. It was way too early for photos.

He stashed the book on a seldom-used bookshelf, then returned to the box for what he thought might help him now. A large clamshell box, like a ring box but much larger, lay within the original box. Dave lifted it out and held it in his hands, turning the velvet-covered box over and over. He looked back at the mark in the floor and recalled the harsh words of the MDA agent.

Shaking his head, he strode toward the bedroom door. Giving up now wouldn't solve a damn thing.

The animal sounds from the bedroom had stopped now. Dave pressed his ear to the door and after a moment could make the distinct sound of sobbing drifting through the wood.

He knocked softly. "Jacqueline? Can I come in?"

There was no response. The sobbing stopped. Dave waited, taking several deep breaths before pushing the door open. The sight of the room reminded Dave of the time he had left a window open during a hurricane. The floor was covered with shredded outfits of all types, including, he realized with a pang, Jacqueline's wedding dress. It was particularly savaged, reduced to tattered sheds of white fabric. In the middle of the devastation was Jacqueline, curled up in the center of the bed, naked, their comforter fashioned into a circular nest. Her tail lay across her muzzle while her spotted coat seemed to shine in the dimming light that streamed through the window.

She did not stir as Dave approached through the sea of fabric and sat on the edge of the bed. "Jacqueline?" He asked very quietly.

"Its all wrong. Everything is wrong." Her voice was a tired whisper.

"I know. I'm sorry." Dave paused. "We'll fix it."

She sniffled a little.

"Jacqueline? May I touch you?" Dave wanted nothing more than to hug her and try to make it all better, but he was afraid of how she'd react to that.

In response she lifted her head and opened her shining amber eyes, the fur around them was soaked with tears. She sighed and then lowered her head back to the bed.

Taking this as permission, Dave crawled forward onto the bed to kneel next to her. He placed a hand on the small of her back and then swept it back along the curve of her spine, stroking her soft fur. After just a few strokes, she sighed and relaxed the curl of her body a bit.

"I'm sorry I snapped at you." It came out a little mumbled,

which Dave recognized as Jacqueline's usual grudging apology and smiled. He started scratching her behind her ears, and after a few strokes she began to press her head up into the fingers. "I'm still mad." Her voice taking on an undertone of a murr.

"I know." Dave said in the practiced tone of a married man, and switched back to stroking her spotted coat, feeling along her spine. Slowly, stroke by stroke, she relaxed the curl of her body and lay flat on her stomach, allowing Dave to run his hand down the entire length of her body. A low rumble began to emanate from her, which Dave felt through his fingers before he heard it. As the purr grew in volume, he could feel the tension drain out from under his fingers as her body relaxed. The final, full-throated purr sounded like a growl but with a soft edge to it. He studied her and looked at the chaos of the room around them. Someday she'd have to face the truth of who she had been and what she was, but not today. Today it was clear she wanted to be the cat. Could he love Jacqueline the Cat? Dave chided himself for asking the question. He already did, he was in here minutes after she nearly tore out his neck.

Dave stopped petting her and leaned down to give her a kiss on the top of her head, between the ears. Then he laid down next to her, dusting his hands free of the fur that clung to it. He made a mental note that they were going to need a much bigger vacuum as he listened to her purr slowly die away.

"You stopped." She said only after her purr had completely faded.

"Several minutes ago. Did you just notice now?" he teased.

She rolled over towards him and nuzzled him; Dave felt her cold nose on his neck, then the roughness of her tongue followed by a more human kiss. The combination of sensation caused a wave of goose bumpsto prickle over Dave's skin. "I didn't tell you to stop."

"You never asked me to start."

In response, she leaned over his chest where his hand was resting, nosed it once and then gave it a hard lick, the sandpaper of her tongue scraping over its tender skin. Dave relented before she licked it again, raising the hand to scratch behind her ears.

Dave chuckled. "A real lady never asks for it, eh?"

Jacqueline did not answer; she just tilted her head to allow Dave's fingers a better angle and closed her shining eyes. She set her head down on his chest and started to purr again. Dave wanted to ask her if she liked the scratching or petting better, but stopped himself. He had accidentally pushed too hard already. Tonight he had to show her he loved her no matter what she was.

He let her stay there for a long while, gently stroking her long hair before he broke the silence. "I got you something."

She popped open one eye. "It had better not be an orange."

Dave chuckled, retrieved the box from the nightstand and placing it in front of her nose. "No worries, this should be neutral in the scent department."

Her eyes widened when the box entered her vision and then pushed herself up onto her knees. Plucking the box off his chest she sniffed it daintily, eyeing it suspiciously. Dave grinned.

"Go ahead and open it. I promise it's safe."

"I am, keep your pants on," she retorted as she fumbled to get a grip on the velvet surface of the box. She resorted to using her claws to pry it open and as she looked inside her jaw dropped. "Oh my god, Dave…" Her amber eyes swiveled to him, full of near disbelief. "Where did you get this?"

"Little birdie sold it to me." Not strictly true, but a not-so-little birdie had delivered it yesterday. It was amazing who and what was on Etsy these days.

Jacqueline lifted what appeared to be a sliver bracelet out of the box. It was inlaid with gold, and on its surface was an etching depicting a jungle filled with leopards and their prey. Gently, she rotated it in her hands, examining all the tiny details as a grin spread over her muzzle, displaying her white fangs to the world around her. "Wow," she breathed as she attempted to slip it onto her wrist, but her paw was far too large to fit through the center. She growled.

"Easy, Jacq. It's not a bracelet."

"Then what is it?" Her words curt.

Dave ignored the tone in her voice and sat up with a confident smirk. "Give it here and turn around."

Those yellow eyes looked at him warily.

"Trust me."

She looked at him for a long moment before sighing, "Alright…" and handing Dave the trinket. She pulled herself off the bed and onto her feet. Then with a last glance at Dave, she spun with a huff and crossed her arms, her tail lashing with annoyance.

Dave caught the tail and she stiffened. "It's not for your wrist, hon." He spoke softly as he inserted the tip of the tail into one end of the bracelet. "It's not something a human could wear." Then, ever so slowly he began to push the ornament up her tail.

Jacqueline gave a mrrowl of surprise as it passed over the thick fur of her tail on its way upward. All the tension slipped from her body as it reached the point where her tail was too wide for it to go any further.

"Not sure how well it will stay." Dave commented as he pushed up on the tail cuff, making sure it was as snug as possible. It sat about four inches from the point where her tail joined with her spine. He sat back and admired it for a moment as Jacqueline twisted her torso to peer at it. The silver accented the golden yellow of her coat and matched the bracelet she still wore from the doctor. Gold trim elevated the ornament from merely eye-catching to exotic. Dave felt a familiar stirring as he let his eyes wander over the fine curve of her spotted hips and buttocks. Jacqueline reached behind her and ran her hand down the length of her tail. Her amber eyes were positively glowing with happiness. It was plain to see that Dave's message had been well received.

"I love it." Her voice said along with a growing purr. "Does it look good?"

Dave coughed, "Well. I suppose that's not something you wear if you want to discourage men from staring at your tail."

"Oh? And what if I want to encourage them?" Her throaty voice was high, teasing. She started to walk away, swinging her hips with a confident strut, her tail mirroring the movement, and as she passed the window the tail cuff glinted in the fading sunlight. Dave shifted uncomfortably on the bed. His complaints about her inhumanness were going to be a distant memory if she was going to act like that. She moved with an effortless grace that radiated a supple and feminine power.

She ended her strut in front of the full-length mirror and spun to examine herself. Looking backwards over her shoulder, she whipped her tail back and forth experimentally. Dave was glad to see her lips part just enough that he could see the glint of her white teeth. He had learned that this somewhat scary expression was her natural smile. She turned back to him as the motion of her tail slowed into slow sinuous lashes that accented a rhythmic sway of her hips.

"It's not the most comfortable thing, as it's bending a ring of fur the wrong way, but it's not slipping. Little heavy but the weight…" she trailed off, closed her eyes and allowed the growing motion of her hips travel up her spine. "Makes me want to dance."

"Dance?" Dave blinked. This was new. Jacqueline told him about dancing way back in high school, but he had never seen her dance himself; occasional weddings where they took turns stepping on each other's toes not withstanding. However if she wanted to put on a show, he certainly wasn't going to complain. He settled into the bed to watch, reflecting on the number of sharp bends the day had taken. "Sure, I'll watch."

She tilted her head forward at just the right angle and something in her deep yellow eyes drove Dave's heart into his throat. Her tongue flicked out of her mouth and ran up the left side of her muzzle. "No," she whispered. "You stand up." She gestured with the tip of a wicked claw that slid from the end of her thick index finger. Dave swallowed, not sure he liked the tone of command, and the sight of that claw touched the memory of the fresh claw marks in wooden flooring. Still, even at her least rational state, she had not actually hurt him. He stood. She growled with approval and beckoned him closer with the claw. Obediently, he took one step forward, and then another and she motioned him to stop. "Good man," Her voice a slow purr.

"Now what? Dave's voice nearly cracked.

"Stay rrright there. Don't move a mmmuscle." She licked her

lips again, Dave wondered if he was in the bedroom with his wife or a hungry animal. "Listen to the music."

"What music?" They didn't even have a stereo in their bedroom.

"You'll hear it." She smiled for a moment; Dave caught the wet glint of her teeth between her lips as her eyes slowly closed. She took a deep breath, visibly centering herself, as her tail began to swish behind her like the pendulum of a clock. Tilting her muzzle upward, exposing the lighter fur of her neck, she let out that breath as the motion of her tail began to creep into her spine. Her hands drifted to her hips, accenting their movement. They'd swing to one side, pulse in, then out and slowly swing to the other side to the beat of an unheard rhythm. Then her paws floated upwards, guiding Dave's eyes up her stomach-- the muscles rippling under her golden spotted pelt-- then to her lower pair of pert breasts, positioned over the lower portion of her slightly elongated rib cage. Dave focused on them as they weaved and swayed just a tad behind the motions of her undulating torso. Her hands crossed in front of them and interlocked in a hypnotic motion, recapturing Dave's eyes. She pulled her hands upwards, through the cleavage of her top breasts, through the fur of her white spotted throat, and over her head where they broke apart. Dave's gaze fell into Jacqueline's eyes. They seemed to emit their own light and shined with such a feral intensity that the part of Dave's brain that still thought it was monkey in a tree began quake in fear of the predator in the room.

Arms out-stretched to either side, she danced in a slow spin, displaying every inch of her beautiful body. The gold of her coat seemed to shine as her hips undulated forward and back, the motion of her body hypnotic. The apartment faded from Dave's vision, until she was a shining point in the darkness. At the very edge of his perception, Dave heard the sound of drums. Like distant thunder at first, but as the dance continued, they grew louder and louder until it sounded like they were in the room with them, surrounding them with the thunderous beats. Jacqueline slowly spun as the tempo carried her. Her hands came inward, cupping her top pair of breasts, her amber eyes opened as a lusty moan escaped her, but she still continued to spin. Each turn, she brought her hands an inch lower until they reached her second pair. She lowered them further, drawing Dave's eyes to the third set of swollen nipples where they pushed out of the thick creamy fur of her belly. She pinched them and let out of low animal moan that seemed to hang in the air. The drums stopped, and Jacqueline opened her eyes, locking them with Dave. He could feel her look into him, probing deep beneath the surface of his mind. Slowly, a smile spread across her muzzle, and her hips, which had stilled when she had pinched herself, began to undulate forward and back with an unmistakable intent.

The drums crept back to life with a soft, slow beat and Jacqueline shifted her dance, starting to put one foot in front of the other and then pause, then another step. She stalked towards him as her tail tip twitched on the beat. Beat by slow, torturous beat, she drew closer until Dave could feel the heat of her breath on his face and taste it in his mouth. The beat swelled as she stood there, an inch away from him. He longed to touch her, to feel her gorgeous, golden fur under his hands, but her inhuman eyes held him tighter than an iron vise. He couldn't move; he could barely breathe. His erection was straining against his pants, and he could feel the wet fibers of his cotton underwear pressing painfully into his sensitive tip. As the beats reached their crescendo her lips inched closer to his. Just as he felt the tips of her lips against his, the beat crested and she pulled away, leaving Dave aching. She stepped past him, her tail curling around his waist as she stepped behind him. Circling him, her tail slithered around his torso like a seductive snake before she pressed herself against his back. Dave shuddered as she gave him a long, slow lick from the base of his neck into his hairline. Want seized him but as he reached behind to touch her, she caught his wrists.

"No," she growled and Dave felt her jaws clamp down on back of his neck. Dave whimpered as he felt her sharp teeth press into his flesh, holding him fast, but not hurting him. The message was clear; when she released his wrists he kept them at his sides. This was a game he recognized, but he was used to being on the other side. The pressure faded into a slow lick as she dragged her rough tongue across his shoulders as her arms encircled his chest. Her claws hooked into the fabric of his shirt and tore it away from his body, exposing his torso to the humid air. Jacqueline danced against him making sure he could feel all six of her rock-hard nipples drag over his skin. Dave panted as she played him like an instrument: the softness of her fur, the coolness of her pads, the prick of her claws and warm roughness of her tongue dancing over his skin.

"Oh, Jacq!" He begged. His body was already screaming for release, but he didn't dare move. She was in control.

"I love you," she purred in his ear as she brought her hand paw up to hold his face. "Do you trust me?"

Dave hesitated and let the question hang before finally whispering, "Yes."

She chuffed in approval and Dave's eyes widened as her claws slid out from the tips of her fingers, each one nearly an inch long and needle-sharp (except for one she had broken at the hospital). "Don't breathe," she commanded. He held his breath as those claws touched his face. Slowly, she dragged them down his face, over his throat, and down his torso. They went through his pants if they were woven of butter and did not withdraw until they reached his ankles. Dave sighed with relief as the fabric fell away.

Relief however, was short lived as Jacqueline began to rub her muzzle against the inside of his legs, Dave gasped, his body starting to shake as she rubbed up and down on his inner thigh. Her long whiskers tickled the leg opposite of the one she touched. Pressure began to build at the base of his shaft before she had even touched it. She shifted from his leg and began to carefully lap at his balls, the hair protecting it somewhat from the abrasive tongue. Dave made a mewling noise of his own as he began to shudder and sweat. "Garr-k-k." Then she reached up and ran a single finger from the base of his cock to the tip. Dave stopped breathing, on the very edge of orgasm. Jacqueline pulled herself up to the side of it and very carefully flicked his tip with the smooth underside of her tongue once, twice and on the third time, Dave came screaming. His white cum streamed out from his tip and arced into the darkness.

Dave collapsed onto his knees, panting and drenched in sweat. A little piece of him felt guilty about blowing it already, but mostly he felt relief. They were done.

That feeling only lasted about twenty seconds before a firm paw pushed him down onto the packed earth. Jacqueline looked down at him, her half lidded eyes radiated warmth. She rowled at him softly, then separated his legs. "Jacq, no. I need-" the sensation of her hand closing around his balls cut off his weak protest. He could only gasp as she leaned down to run her tongue from the inside of his knee to his crotch. His sweat lubricated his skin so that the rough tongue produced an entirely different sensation from the pain he had expected. A second lick, just to the left of the first, made the leg tremble. "Jacq, that really-- Aught! Sensitive." Jacqueline gave no sign of hearing him and continued to lap at his salty skin, working her way up his body with torturous slowness.

Jacqueline kept her neck straight as she groomed her writhing mate, driving her tongue with her entire body, her fur teasing Dave's skin as she moved up and down. As she reached the bottom of his rib cage, she pushed herself against him, enveloping his slightly flaccid cock in the softness of her cleavage. Then with a lick that went from the base of his sternum to the very tip of his chin, she ground the flagging member along entire length of her torso, making him moan out loud. The stiffness of his erection was completely restored as she ground back the other way. She repeated this maddening maneuver twice before Dave could no longer restrain himself. His hands reached up and clutched at her top breasts just as her tongue lifted from the side of his neck; they were soft and firm in his hands. She growled in pleasure and continued to push herself up his body. Dave felt the wet kiss of the lips of her pussy as she dragged herself over his cock. In response, Dave's fingers found her swollen nipples and gave them a savage twist. Jacqueline roared in response, her body went rigid and Dave twisted the other way. Her lips parted, making a loose 'O' as she pushed away from him, sitting up on his stomach, pulling her breasts out of reach. Undeterred, Dave let his hand travel down her chest and wrapped his hands around her lower pair, rubbing his thumbs against these nipples. Her tail curled around his left leg as she moaned with pleasure. Slowly, she brought her hand-paws up and closed her thick fingers around his wrists. She allowed Dave to tease her a moment longer before reluctantly peeling his hands from her breasts and pinning them to the ground on either side of his head. Dave felt the wet chill of her nose against the tip of his own as her eyes loomed in his vision, glowing like twin moons.

She kissed him then, driving her tongue deep into his mouth, wrapping around his own like a constrictor snake. Dave pushed back the best he could and ran his tongue along the sharp ridges of her teeth. A hungry growl ripped through her, and she slowly withdrew, making sure he felt every inch of her tongue as she extracted it from his mouth. They were again nose to nose, their breath intermixing in the humid air of the jungle around them. She was slowly grinding herself against him, teasing him with the fleeting softness of her tail as it flicked between his inner thighs. She was the only thought in Dave's head. His entire body ached for this beautiful creature. Wanting nothing more than to take her, make her scream in pleasure, fill her with himself. Every press against him made him shiver with desire. She leaned down a millimeter and licked him from the base of his chin to the tip of his nose

Dave growled as his self-control snapped. He wanted her NOW! He pushed upward with all the strength he could muster. His wrists rose from the earth one, two, three inches from the ground. His arms shook from the effort and he opened his eyes to her sly grin. "Naughty," she whispered right before she slammed his wrists back to earth without any apparent effort. "But perhaps I've teased you enough?" She slid backwards, moving the wet lips of her vagina down the length of his shaft. Dave squeaked and thrust against her. She rowled in response, sitting up and positioning Dave's wrist on his chest as she allowed him to thrust against her. Her lips parted as he continued, her pink tongue peeking out over her bottom lip as Dave felt her juices drip around his cock. Then, without warning, she lifted herself off him, allowing his dick to stick into the air, straining for her. Jacqueline looked down between her legs, checking the alignment, and then she slammed herself down, impaling herself on his thick shaft. Both of them screamed in pleasure, Dave found himself thrust deep into the depths of her very tight sex.

Smiling down at him Jacqueline leaned back and let go of his wrists so she was positioned straight above him. Using her huge thigh muscles, she began to slide herself up and down Dave's cock. She started slowly, teasingly, inching herself up and down, but before long she lost herself and began to increase her pace. Animal growls and inhuman screams erupted from her as she pounded herself against Dave, who thrust upwards with as much strength as he could muster. She roared with pleasure as she came the first time, her tail lashing behind her, whipping against the inside of his legs. Dave felt her close around him, squeezing him even tighter than before, making him feel every inch of her as she slid him in and out of her. The sensation made Dave gasp. An incredible amount of pressure began to build at the base of his cock as her tempo increased. She drove herself down onto him again and again. Her own hands playing over her bouncing breasts, grabbing at her nipples one by one, until she reached her hidden, sensitive nipples on her belly. Twisting them, she let loose an almost dog-like howl that made the darkness ripple as Dave felt her spasm around him. Dave barely noticed though, as his own pressure had blotted out any other thoughts as he clutched at Jacqueline's knees, the only hand holds he could find to brace himself in her sexual storm.

Just he was about to burst, as his breath had begun to shudder and slick sweat was pouring from his pores, Jacqueline shifted. She slowed her pace from an animal abandon to a gentle rhythm, letting Dave feel the contours of her inner wall slip around him. It was an utterly torturous sensation, just enough to keep him right on the edge.

She leaned over him, letting her breasts tease his chest, her breath hot on his face. "What do you want, Dave?" Her grin was wicked, mischievous and sexy all at the same time. Dave recognized the question: it was a game they played sometimes in bed, except he was usually the one on top.

"C-come on, Jacq! F-Finish it!" He managed to get out. His body shook with tension, preventing him from making any movement of his own to sate the mind-bending pressure that was continuing to build within him.

"Can't hear you." She whispered as bent her lips to his chest and flicked her tongue over one of his nipples.

Dave screamed, "Let me cum! Please Jacq!" Begging made a small part of him flush with shame, but this was no time for pride. He was rewarded with a slight increase in her tempo. She placed her paws on either side of his head and Dave found himself staring deep into her eyes. They seemed to swirl with a sort of feral intensity, boring into him. Each thrust of her hips drove her gaze deeper into his soul. Dave felt her wrap around his very core, his heart.

"Who's are you?" she growled. There was only answer to her question.

"I'm yours," Dave panted with growing desperation. Something inside him gave way and there was a fleeting impression of a chain, but far more importantly Jacqueline's tempo had increased. He wrapped his arms around her thick, inhuman neck and buried his face in her fur. "I'm yours," he repeated desperately in her ear.

"Damn right you're MINE!" she roared in response as she slammed down into him, driving his cock deep into her sex. Dave bit down on the loose skin of her neck as his body locked up with the tension of the oncoming freight train of an orgasm. Something inside himself twisted as she raised herself up for another slam. Then, in the split second when she was at the top of that arc, something happened; he felt her. Not just her in his arms, but he felt Jacqueline as if he occupied her body. He felt the fur anchored to her skin, the wild sensation of having a tail, the rippling power of her muscles and, most of all, he felt her pussy as if it was his own as it slammed down on his cock. They exploded as one; his scream joining her primal yowl as their hot seed filled their deepest reaches.

They collapsed together onto the bedroom floor, panting in perfect unison. Dave's awareness slowly retracted back into his own body. He lay there for a long moment clutching his wife. No thoughts came to him; his physical exhaustion blotted them out. Finally, he was stirred from his stupor by a cheek lick and Jacqueline's lips on his ear. "I love you."

He turned and kissed her. Her fur smelled damp with his sweat as he touched her forehead to his. "I love you," he said, meaning it with every fiber of his being even as terror began to bubble in the back of his brain. There was no possible way to deny the truth that had been in Dr. Christhof's ranting. The link between him and Jacqueline was more than emotion now; it was a soul binding. Something that only the Fey were capable of.

The woman he loved was a Fey.

CHAPTER 9

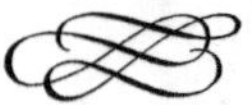

SHATTER

JACQUELINE HAD BEEN HALF AWARE OF THE SOFT SOUNDS OF DAVE getting ready for work for some time before the lids of her eyes cracked open. She had no idea how she had gotten from the floor onto the bed during the night, but she was glad she had. The mattress, while square instead of her kind's preferred circular bedding, was far more comfortable than the floor.

Dave was in the bathroom brushing his teeth, and she watched him through the mirror along the wall. Of course, if she could see him, he could see her. Jacqueline uncurled herself and stretched, arching her back just so a sunbeam caught the white fur of her chest. The sight of Dave freezing mid-brushstroke was immensely satisfying. Through the link she had forged between them, she could feel his eyes rove up her spotted torso, over the curve of her breasts and linger on her dark nipples. She growled at him softly, giving him a little pulse from her hips before rolling away from him.

Within a few moments, she felt his fingers stroking her hair and his voice came to her ears. "Is that a blatant play for attention I see?"

"Maybe," she purred back as his fingers found a sweet spot at

64

the base of her ear. She rolled back onto her back to regard her lover with her bright amber eyes. Dave smiled down on her. Jacqueline pawed at his arm with a seductive smirk. "Murrowl. Come back to bed; I have a much larger itch for you to scratch."

His face darkened and a tiny frown appeared on Dave's lips. "I gotta go to work, hon."

"Awww, but it's my second day home." Judging from the swirling mixture of emotions that were leaking out of him, Jacqueline knew she could probably entice him back into bed if she put a might more effort in, but there'd certainly be trouble later. Dave was a contractor, and if he didn't show up, he didn't get paid. Jacqueline wasn't precisely sure how long she'd been in the hospital, but doubted that the bill was going to be pretty.

Dave snorted and set his jaw. "Besides, after last night I'm not sure I can take much more of your attention."

Jacqueline did her best to look innocent, but her predatory face didn't really communicate the expression well, and it at appeared as a half-hearted pout. "I was just a little… frustrated last night."

"I'm not talking about the bruises. It's not nice to bind your husband."

"But its just a little teeny weenie bond. It doesn't do much, just…" she reached up, clasped his arm and gave it a nip. "…Makes sure everyone knows that you're mine." She playfully gnawed on the captive arm.

"Hey! Let go!" Dave exclaimed and tugged on his arm. Jacqueline growled possessively and flipped him over herself into the bed. He flailed comically as he landed with a thump. "Ack! Jacq! I gotta go to work."

She knew that, but Jacqueline decided he wasn't getting away from her without a little more teasing. "Are you sure you don't have time to pet a certain pussy?" she purred in his ear. Cheesy line, but judging from Dave's shudder it put his mind right where it was supposed to.

He gave her a long, hungry glance before sighing and rolling away to the opposite side of the bed to Jacqueline's disappointment.

"I want you to undo the bond, Jacqueline." He said, while straightening his clothes. "If anybody sees it, there will be questions."

"What? No." In truth, the setting of the bond had been fairly instinctual. She wasn't entirely sure how she had done it, let alone how to remove it. "It's… more fair this way."

"It's fair to claim ownership on your husband? Honey, I don't know what you're thinking but the MDA views any sort of soul bind as dangerous."

Jacqueline's eyes narrowed, not liking his tone or his paranoia. The link was mostly harmless. She could tell roughly where he was, his emotional state and if he was healthy through it. He was adept-- a magic perceptive-- he should be able to see that their link was about as malevolent as a lady bug. "You're mine David. If you're going to own me legally, then I'm staking my own claim on you." She was crouching on the bed now, a faint growl rising in her throat.

David flinched as if slapped. "I-I didn't have any choice about that."

"So which am I, Dave? Your child or your pet?" Jacqueline could feel that she was being unreasonable, but it felt wrong to question the soul bond. It felt like the most natural thing in the world to do. How she had NOT bonded Dave after four years of marriage was puzzling, but unimportant for the moment.

Dave bit his lip and took a deep breath, not meeting her eyes. "Alright, point taken. We'll talk about this when I get home." He looked up at her after a moment of silence. "Will you be okay here, today?"

Jacqueline huffed and rolled over so that her back was facing him. "I'll be fine. I'll just lay here all day like a good little kitty." Her gravelly voice box seeped the words in a sarcastic coating.

Silence. Then, "I love you."

Jacqueline's tail twitched and then she echoed the words softly-- just loud enough for him to hear as he exited the room. A few minutes later, she heard the front door open and then shut with a bang. She winced, there had to have been better ways to handle the situation that was for sure. Feeling guilty, she curled herself into a tight ball and sighed. Some homecoming.

Jacqueline lingered in bed as long as her body would allow. The apartment, which was both familiar and unfamiliar at the same time, gave her an uneasy feeling. She was not particularly eager to find more surprises like her closet. Finding a full wardrobe of human clothing, along with a faint scent of a human woman in her closet had really driven her over the edge while she was still reeling from the sheer insanity of orange-tainted ham. She could smell that woman even now. It was an old smell, to be sure, but it seemed to saturate everything. Why did her apartment reek of a human woman? It must have something to do with her accident but that train of thought threatened her with a migraine of pain. She busied herself with grooming the remains of Dave's sweat out of her fur, focusing on him, and trying to push all the uncomfortable questions out of her head for now.

It was her stomach that finally forced her from her nest. It reminded her in a very loud manner that she hadn't eaten since they had left the hospital. With a sigh, she padded out of the bedroom and into the kitchen.

The kitchen looked as she remembered, if a bit more disorganized from enduring at least two weeks of Dave's mismanagement. However, that sense of familiarity ended as soon as she wrapped her handpaw around the handle of the refrigerator door, it felt uncomfortably thin to her, and that was only the beginning. The baggy that had an untouched steak in it slipped from her clumsy fingers and splatted on the floor twice. The microwave frustrated her so much with its tiny control pad that Jacqueline felt the need to redecorate it with some claw marks. Fortunately the unit was fairly study and eventually agreed to warm her steak.

It was well past noon by the time she had finished breakfast and trekked into the bathroom to begin her day. Habit carried her into the shower and guided her hands to the water spigot before she realized what she was doing and stopped herself. She had already spent an hour grooming, she didn't need a shower! Shaking her head, she went to the sink and brushed her teeth with what felt like an impossibly small toothbrush. At least at the hospital they had given her a much larger one. After spitting and lapping at the faucet a few times to get the horrible taste off her tongue, she reached up and opened the medicine cabinet. Three entire shelves of useless, human makeup stared back at her.

Snarling, she slammed the cabinet closed and stalked from the bathroom, thoughts whirling. Just how long had she been away? Why had there been a *human* woman living with Dave? How could he do such a thing to her? Didn't he love her? Jacqueline could feel the rage slipping over her mind like a protective blanket. She looked around the bedroom and bared her teeth at its false familiarity. Oh sure, it appeared to be her bedroom, but where were all the pictures? You could see the outline of a few of them on the walls, the unfaded paint betraying their absence.

It was as if somebody had been living HER life, living with HER mate and she had been replaced wholesale. Where were her things? Where were her mementos from her jungle home? Where was her LIFE?

CRACK! Jacqueline slammed the closest thing with both paws, and the top of her dresser split cleanly in half. Snarling with frustration, she tore the top of the dresser off and hurled it against the wall where it made a very satisfying crunch as the plaster buckled from the impact. Growling, Jacqueline, turned back to the dresser and saw what was in the top drawer.

Underwear! The drawer was stuffed full of underwear. She didn't even wear underwear! It was hard enough to remember clothing half the time! Yet her eyes were drawn to a flash of color: a hot pink bra and panty set with long, matching satin gloves and stockings. She had made sure Dave's birthday had been fun last year. She picked it up, sniffed it and roared with pain as she felt a white hot spike of pain stab her between the eyes! It SMELLED LIKE HER! The interloper! Impossible! Jacqueline remembered wearing it and yet the bra was too big and there was no second cup! AND...! AND...!

Clutching her head, Jacqueline reeled back from the dresser shouting curses intermixed with inhuman sounds. It felt as if something was constricting her brain. She tried to flee for the door but, blinded by pain, she slammed headlong into the doorframe, knocking herself to the floor. Panic took over; she sprung up on all fours and dashed into the living room, trying to get away, trying to hide from the pain. Where could she go? She clawed at the front door, yowling at it to open, but it held despite the gashes she tore in it. The pain continued. She could still scent the presence of the interloper here. Kitchen? Worse. Her office sent her reeling anew. Dave's study? Just Dave there, no interloper, no fake, human her. Nothing but Dave's chair, desk and computer. It all smelled like Dave and no one else. That was the one shred of comfort she had as she huddled under the desk in the closet of a room and wept.

The horrible pain eventually subsided, but the confusion did not. Her tears kept spilling from her eyes and soaked into her facial fur, turning it into a wet mess. What was going on? Why was every thing so wrong? Why couldn't she remember? These thoughts just ran in circles in her head, going nowhere. She should call Dave tell him to stop cheating on her. If he was, but...

The doorbell buzzed, disrupting her spiral of thought. She sniffed and lifted her head from her huddle to face the sound, not sure if the sound had been real. It buzzed again, seemingly insistent. Hesitantly, she began to crawl out from under the desk, her tail drooping with her uncertainty. Again the sound rolled through the apartment. Steeling herself, Jacqueline pushed up onto two feet and went to answer the door. She checked the peephole, saw no one and cautiously opened the door a crack. There, laid carefully on the doormat, was a beautiful golden collar.

As soon as she saw it Jacqueline knew it was hers. Her neck felt bare-- it needed to feel the collar's weight. Picking it up, Jacqueline felt a flow of comforting warmth wash over her. The aching of her shoulder where she had plowed into the bedroom door melted away. The collar's finely wrought chains seemed to whisper to her. It promised to take her away and protect her from the pain. Her throat rumbled with a purr as she undid the clasp and brought the collar to her neck.

That's when something BIT her. Burning pain roared into her

wrist, and Jacqueline whirled, dropping the collar as she readied her claws to attack. No one was there. Spitting with anger she swiped at the air but her claws met no invisible attacker. Instead, something on her wrist left a streak of color across her vision. The stone on her bracelet, the one Dr. Niddler gave her, was glowing bright red. That meant something. Something important. Jacqueline wracked her brain, which suddenly seemed to be full of fog. Red meant glamour. Very hostile. Mind-altering glamour. Slowly, she brought her gaze down to the collar crumpled at her feet. Pain flared in her wrist again, but it was duller, bearable. A warning. The collar looked far more aged than it had a moment ago, its metal dull and in need of cleaning. There was a tag on it, declaring the bearer of the collar to be the property of someone called Menzo. She wasn't sure who that was, but the name made her cold. He had something to do with her accident, she was sure of that.

She had to get out of there. Leaving the collar where it had fallen, she reached back into the apartment to grab her keys and then took off down the hallway. She bounded down three flights of stairs, making an unsuspecting neighbor scatter groceries everywhere after a near collision. She reached her car and threw open the door. It stank of the interloper, but she had no time to worry about that now. She was just thankful that the car was an automatic, because her foot-paws were too large to handle three pedals. After far too much futzing to adjust the seat, Jacqueline peeled out of the parking lot and onto the road.

There was no destination in her mind; Jacqueline just drove. She wove through traffic haphazardly, trying to stay calm despite the paranoia that was creeping in on her.

She only realized that she was done driving when she pulled into a parking lot for one of the state forest hiking trails on the edge of town. Yes, that made sense to her. The perfect place to get away from both her apartment and sinister jewelry for a while.

Stashing the key under the front tire of her car, Jacqueline strode into the forest wearing nothing but two pieces of jewelry and her spots. The light breeze felt good on her uncovered body. She was free of the hospital and those silly gowns. Free of people pressing her with expectations of proper behavior. Free of trying to be something she was not. At least for a little while.

Jacqueline had no map and no watch, so she just walked along the forest trails, giving no heed to any posted signs. Occasionally, she passed a wide-eyed hiker, but she paid them no mind. After some time, a shift began to come about in her. A sound or scent would attract her attention, and she would instinctively fall to all fours, alert-- ears scanning the forest. Three times this occurred, and she climbed back onto two legs and shook herself. The fourth time she didn't bother, and allowed her instincts to lead from the path and into a low valley.

Letting her instincts guide her was easy. Breakfast was a distant memory and it had been hours since she had eaten. The forest was full of stupid deer that watched for two-legs who carried death in a stick, but they had forgotten to fear hunters that slunk low to the ground on four paws. There was a scent on the breeze that made Jacqueline's mouth water. The musky scent of a male deer. She crept in its direction hoping the wind would not change.

The deer proved to be closer than she could have hoped. He was young and lean, but there was ample meat on his bones to make him worth the effort. The soil was soft and silent under her paws-- the dampness of the spring season aiding her stealth.

The poor beast had no chance. So focused on nibbling on the tender shoots of new growth that it didn't notice Jacqueline until she only six feet away. Her powerful legs launched her into the air, her claws sinking into his right flank, and he fell to the ground with a pathetic bleat. Jacqueline scrambled over its thrashing form, grabbed his small rack and held it to the ground as she clamped her jaws on his throat. It took a surprisingly long time for the stubborn thing's lungs to fail and lay still.

Grinning, Jacqueline tore the deer's stomach open and began to gorge herself on the soft organ meats. There was nothing quite like burying your muzzle in the still warm entrails of a kill and gulping down a succulent liver. Cooked meat had its place, but not much could beat raw, bloody and warm. She ate until her stomach literally bulged with meat. Her muzzle, paws and front were soaked with blood by the time she finished. Afterwards, she regarded the corpse with an appraising eye as she cleaned off her paws.

The young buck had been healthy and fairly large, maybe a hundred pounds or so. Judging from the bulge in her torso and the mess she had made, she had probably eaten ten pounds. There was enough left there to feed her for a couple weeks. She would just have to butcher it and stick it in a freezer. Now she just had to drag it up a tree and…

Jacqueline grabbed the carcass and looked around for a likely spot and then blinked. That couldn't be right. It would rot. She looked back at the deer's glazed eye. Bury it instead? No, that was ridiculous. Mom and Dad would never approve of wasting that much meat. Jacqueline winced. That now familiar spike of pain was coming back, and this time driving through the back of her skull. This… couldn't be right. She remembered her mother butchering plenty of kills, but for the life of her couldn't recall how. The pain increased and she whimpered, she clawed at the air trying to ward it off.

She should know how to field dress a kill, she must have done it hundreds of times unless…

Mom hated blood. Fainted at the sight of it, but that made no sense. She was a leopard, too, unless…

With each thought, the pain increased. She fell to the forest floor, moaning and whimpering. But there was nowhere left for her thoughts to go.

Dave had been living with a human for years, but SHE had lived with him. That made no sense unless…

Why hadn't she bonded Dave to her long ago? It would have made sense unless…

Nothing felt right in her hands. Everything she touched was unfamiliar, but she would have used them hundreds of times.

Unless, unless, unless… A series of images, contradictions, just kept piling on her like someone building a stack of bricks on her brain. She felt something within herself beginning to crack.

Then it all gave way.

The forest was filled with a sound it had never heard before.

Somewhere between a human scream and a cat's roar, it embodied pain beyond most mortal measures. It went beyond sound as it swept through the forest and out into the town. Every living creature that had eyes turned in the direction of it and shuddered. One immediately started to head in the direction of the sound, but he was far away.

CHAPTER 10

HUNTING FOR THE HUNTRESS

Dave was not at work. He, in fact, had never intended on going to work. That had all been part of the plan. The plan, as far he was concerned, had taken a wrong turn and somehow wound up in the middle of Hiroshima just in time for the Fat Boy to fall on its head. Dave was cursing himself as he walked through the forest; the baleful mutters seemed to darken the forest around him.

He should have listened to Dr. Niddler and let Jacqueline stay in the hospital for six months. Sure the medical bills would have bankrupted the both of them, but maybe Jacqueline would be sane. Well, sane enough that Dave wouldn't fear being eaten in his own home. But noooo! He had decided to use a folk remedy he found on the Internet to break the spell. After all, it was just variation of Dr. Niddler's confrontation therapy, but instead of throwing a single stone of reality every day, you hit them with a wrecking ball of their former life. Hide photographs and make the bewitched live in the old environment, and wait for the glamor to shatter. Simple. Whoever wrote the page obviously was not dealing with a woman who had sprouted fangs, claws and had packed on twenty additional pounds of muscle.

There had been plenty of signs that this was a bad idea. The fact that Jacqueline had soul bound him last night was the icing on the cake. As far as he knew, humans were not supposed to even be capable of that. It was pure Fey magic-- used in their social hierarchy. Which, if Jacqueline could preform it, meant that she was far more Fey than Dr. Niddler had suspected. That should have been clue number one to pack Jacqueline up and take her back to the hospital. Instead he hustled off to the local coffee shop and stuck to the plan.

It had started off promising; he had watched her start her day through the various hidden cameras he had placed throughout the apartment. She had confronted the strangeness of her surroundings, suffered a breakdown and retreated to the one place in the house that she had the least memories of. That was all in the plan. Then somebody had rung the fucking doorbell and everything had gone straight to kablooie land. Dave wasn't sure what had happened at the door, but it hadn't even occurred to him to take her car keys with him this morning. Even after sprinting back to the apartment building, he'd only managed to catch a glimpse of her car turning the corner. It was only through the use of the accursed link he'd manage to find her at all once he retrieved his own car, but that failed, too, once they reached the edge of town. It was as if she had just faded into a cloud as she exited the highway.

Fortunately, there were only a few destinations off that particular exit, and after looking for her car at the sportsman store and the bowling alley, that left the national forest. The national forest with about fifty different parking lots in different locations along its trails. There was no choice but to check them all, one by one.

By the time he found the car, she was long gone. Sick with worry, Dave had headed into the forest without a thought. Forests were tuned to the Fey world; even secondary growth forests like this one. If Jacqueline stumbled into an entryway, Dave might lose his love forever. All because he had been worried about a stupid thing like bankruptcy. Doubts nagged at him, the voice of the MDA guy was particularly loud in his mind. It told him not only that the plan was stupid, but also that loving the creature his wife had become was impossible. This new Jacqueline was so much more than she had been-- wild and full of energy when happy, and capable of terrible rage when upset. Last night, when she had dominated him, had been both thrilling and pants-wettingly terrifying. Maybe she would eat him and consume his bones someday. He finally told his doubts to shut the hell up and hurried onto a trail.

He hiked along the myriad paths for hours, watching the underbrush for any sign of movement. Everyone he passed was asked if they had seen a Leopard Woman walk this way. They all looked at him as if he was nuts. He had to concede that it was a possibility. Dave didn't care; he had to fix this somehow, some way.

That was when he felt her. He had been walking for more than two hours before the link between them roared to life after being clouded. Jacqueline was in pain-- great, mind-blowing pain. Only a small portion of it squeezed through the link, but that was enough to make Dave stagger and fall to his knees. Then heard her scream. It was a sound midway between animal and human, but all pain. Dave's heart began to thunder. Someone was hurting his wife! He felt her now. Whatever had been blocking the link had been burned away.

"Hang on, hon. I'm coming." The forest seemed to take his promise with silent assent as he turned around, now realizing that he had taken the path heading away from Jacqueline. He cursed his utter lack of tracking skills.

CHAPTER 11

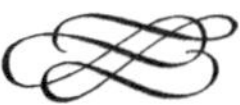

CONSEQUENCES

JACQUELINE DID NOT DARE TO MOVE. HER HEAD FELT FULL OF broken glass, and the slightest movement made it shift. Despite the pain, her mind was clear. The forced reordering of her memories, that presence in her head, all that was gone. Opening her eyes, Jacqueline looked down her short muzzle and into the high branches of the trees that blocked the sky, then let out a slow, shuddering breath.

She could have lain there for a while; just breathing as she waited for the dulling memories of the pain to fade, but someone nearby started a slow, heavy clap. Jacqueline had no doubt about who was that someone was. She pushed herself upright, wincing at the renewed pain in her head as she found Menzo. He was about thirty feet away, leaning against a tree trunk with an easy grace. His clothes were quite different from last time. He had shed the tux in favor of a medieval style tunic and breeches. The shirt was open, showing a muscular chest, and his sculpted face possessed an elegance that bordered on the inhuman-- too symmetrical, perfect. He grinned at Jacqueline through clenched teeth as he brought his hands together in a perfectly on-beat clap.

"Very impressive, Jacqueline! Not many could break a glamour like that."

Jacqueline felt as if she was being sized up as his eyes swept over her body. She also noted that his hand fell to rest on the hilt of a thin sword that hung from his waist.

A growl rose from Jacqueline's throat as she pushed herself off the ground. "Leave me alone. I want nothing to do with you."

He shook his head and frowned. "I am afraid it's a little late for that. You are not a bored little secretary anymore. You are both my creation and my responsibility. I have come to take you home."

Having found her feet, Jacqueline held up her paw to him and unsheathed her wickedly sharp claws. The sight of them made Menzo tense and Jacqueline felt hope that this encounter would not be as one-sided as the first. "I am not going to be owned by you or anyone else, Menzo."

"Everyone is owned by something or someone, Jacqueline. It is our nature. Your nature. Just ask Dave."

The memories of the night and her pure NEED to bind Dave to herself last night came flooding back and her ears flattened against her head. "No." She paused, mentally forcing the waver from her voice. "I'm not like you. I am not a Fey."

He chuckled; it was far lower than expected for a man of his small size. "You are not even remotely human, my pet. No glamour remains on your body or mind, but the spots remain."

Stealing a glance at herself, it was true, blood soaked fur clung to the six breasts that hung on her chest. She could feel her tail wave behind her, the weight of the tail cuff a comforting weight on her spine. It was real. She was not human.

When her eyes rose back to Menzo, he was holding something in his hand, but she couldn't make it out. The air around it seemed to ripple with heat, shielding it from her eyes. Menzo grinned, showing his perfectly straight, white teeth as he extended his palm and the thing toward her. Jacqueline took a step away. "Do you recognize this, Jacqueline?"

Jacqueline did not, but there was a sense of familiarity to it. As her eyes fought to focus on it, Jacqueline was struck with a sense of disconnection between her and her body. All the differences between it and her old body bubbled into her consciousness-- its new supple power and flexibility, the alterations to her base instincts, and now more fight than flight. The discarding of any tendency to submit to her husband. The thing pined for her, wordlessly telling her that she should be human, that her current form was wrong. "What is that thing!?" Jacqueline hissed. Her ears went flat against her head and her skin prickled with the rising of her fur.

"Why, its your humanity, Jacqueline, which you discarded with all the sorrow of scratching off a tick or flea. Wouldn't you like it back now? It would make your life so much easier. You could go back to your job. I would leave you alone, and your husband will love you again." He took a step forward, holding the thing out towards Jacqueline. She snarled defensively and took a step back.

The mere thought of becoming human again filled Jacqueline with a hackle-rising dread. Jacqueline was shocked at the strength of her revulsion, but it was there, plain as day. She'd rather die than give up her spots. "Dave--," she tried to focus again on the little man in front of her. "Dave loves me as I am."

Menzo just smiled as he took another step toward her. "Does he, Jacqueline? Does he really? He loved the human Jacqueline. He says he loves you out of duty to the memory of her, not you. He fears you, thinks that you have a *disease*. What will happen when he realizes that you chose to be a monster?"

"I--I didn't..." the words trailed off into a confused growl, and Menzo brought that thing in his hand closer.

"Go ahead. Take your humanity back, then. It's right here, Jacqueline. I'm offering you the same choice as before, no tricks. Not a trick. Not a trick. Not a trick." Three times meant it was true.

Jacqueline's eyes flicked to the stone on her wrist and then back to Menzo. It was black; there was no glamour here. She prodded the depths of her mind. The shattered glamour was still there, but inert, swept into a dark corner where images of her human life were distorted into life as a leopard. She imagined herself human again, and shuddered. The thought of giving up the sensations of her form, going through life with muffled human senses, no quiet hum of magic in her mind, or even the sensation of blood drying under her claws. No. For good or for ill, this creature was what she was supposed to be. Logic be damned. This was her now. She'd fight for this. Dave would adjust or he wouldn't. That would be his choice. This was hers.

"It can whither and die. I am what I want to be. I am what I am supposed to be." Her gravelly voice rang with a note that buzzed in her ears and faded into the forest around them. A note answered her, and both she and Menzo blinked in surprise. The thing in his hand gave a warbling note of grief and unraveled into nothingness.

Menzo looked at his hand as he rubbed his thumb against his forefingers in circular motion as if feeling something slick on his fingers. "Well, that was a little harsh. Wielding a truth like that against the little thing." He shrugged and then flashed Jacqueline a dangerous grin. "You've made your choice then, my lovely monster. Let's talk consequences, shall we?" He turned his head to the side and called out to the forest, "Come on out, Jasper!"

Jacqueline's ears, then her eyes zeroed in on a rustling in the nearby undergrowth. Then her jaw fell open as she watched a spotted creature emerge from a thicket that had been far to small to conceal it. Muscles rippled under the fur of his broad back as he strode forward effortlessly on pad-like hands that resembled Jacqueline's own, except larger. Everything about this leopard man was massive, rivaling that of a tiger. The yellow of his fur shined with health as he stalked toward Menzo with a confident swagger. Menzo placed his hand paternally on the beast's head and his grin grew. "Spring is such a wonderful time of the year isn't it, Jacqueline?"

Jacqueline was so distracted that she didn't hear him, her mind focused on Jasper with the intensity of a laser. Heat rose within her. It started between her legs and crept up into her body, filling her and making breathing difficult. Trying to steady herself, she shook her head and drew a deep breath through her nose, also drawing in a thick musky scent that had not been in the air a moment ago. It flowed into her head and coated her mind with carnal thoughts that instantly hardened all six of her nipples. Without thinking her paws rose to her top breasts and squeezed, she could feel them swelling

under her paws, becoming firm and pert. "What," she gasped. "What did you d--" her voice trailed off to a soft moan as all her breasts expanded, stretching their sensitive skin as they each gained a full cup size.

"Jasper here has just reminded your body of what it should be doing at this time of the year." The huge leopard growled enticingly and circled around Menzo, displaying his long muscular body for Jacqueline. Her mind slowly pried the visual details of his form from his gorgeous whole. His shoulders and arms were structured so that he could indeed stand on two legs if he so chose. His eyes, ice blue human orbs, locked with her own inhuman eyes. Lust burned within them, making Jacqueline desperately want to perform a much more intimate inspection on Jasper body. "Do you like what you see, Jacqueline?" Menzo's voice seemed far, far away.

"Oh yes." There was no denying it. Jacqueline practically panted with lust.

"He could be yours, Jacqueline. I'd give him to you if you returned with me. In fact," Menzo gave the big cat an affectionate ear scratch. "Why do don't you give her a little taste, Jasper."

The deep rumble of agreement that rolled from Jasper made Jacqueline's heart miss a beat. It pounded in her ears as he slinked toward her, her eyes drinking in the mouth-watering beauty that he seemed to secrete. Jacqueline's tail lifted of its own volition as he flowed towards her, its tip brushing the back of her head. She shifted uncomfortably as she fought the urge to join him on all fours, to present herself to him. He was a trap, but oh god, was he a beautiful one, and she could not bring herself to escape. She trembled at his touch as he rubbed the length of his entire body against her, his thick tail curling around her torso as he stepped past her. Jacqueline caught it and pressed it to herself, moaning as she felt it pass under her swollen lower breasts. His scent was heavenly. She put her fingers to her muzzle to taste it, feeding her want and need.

Menzo's voice intruded, "You'll never have to worry about breaking this one. He can take whatever you give, and give you what ever you want."

His voice reminded her of the danger, the trap. Vibrating with effort, she forced her legs together and tried to ignore the wet feeling between them.

"Show her, Jasper. Show her how you can make her feel." Menzo's voice had a pitch of child-like glee that made a small portion of Jacqueline's remaining higher brain functions scream at her to get away but her body wanted no part of running.

Jasper was circling her now, teasing her with the lightest of contact of his thick fur against hers. He circled once, twice, three times. Each time, Jacqueline thrust her chest out more and lifted her tail even higher. She raked her claws through his pelt, and on the end of that third circle, when he nosed the damp triangle of fur between her legs, Jacqueline's legs parted ever so slightly. There was a triumphant smirk on his muzzle as he pressed into her to give her sex a long, slow lap. Jacqueline made a sound that was like a cross between a kitten's cry and the hiss of escaping gas.

He licked her again and her body shivered. The tongue was smooth against her wet sex and seemed to be coated with a pure pleasure that rocketed up into her body. She wanted more, and squatted to allow him better access. Jasper rumbled in approval, starting to lap at her in earnest. Some small reserve of willpower tried to push him away, but it could not muster any strength into her arms. He pushed forward, forcing Jacqueline to hold on to his ears to keep upright and keep that magical tongue as close as possible. Every long lap brought a new bolt of pleasure, that did not fade, but spread through her entire body, charging every cell of her being. She could feel the breeze on every fur follicle, every sensation seemed to add to the rushing tidal wave coursing through her, but it gave no sign of crashing.

Yet there was one spot that was not singing with the orgasmic chorus. Pain stabbed through the pleasure-- her wrist-- and her nostrils caught a whiff of singeing flesh even as she ground against Jaspers muzzle, his long, smooth tongue finding its way deep inside her. She forced her eyes open a hair, and was nearly blinded by the fiery glare of the gem of her bracelet. Glamour. She was caught in a dangerous glamour. Menzo. Where was he?

Something brushed her neck fur, encircling it. She tried to twist away, but Jasper reached up with those hand-paws and dug his claws into her flanks, holding her in place. There was a heavy click and Jacqueline felt a chill close around her heart.

"There. You are mine, Jacqueline." Menzo cooed in her ear as he snatched the bracelet from her wrist. "I've collared you fairly."

"F-F-Fuck off and D-DiAAAHHRRRG!!" Jacqueline cried out in pain as she felt the bone chilling cold of her master's disapproval slice through her heart. Master? Her mind fled that traitorous thought, focusing instead on the incredible pleasure flowing up from Jasper. She opened her legs wider, allowing him to drive that magic tongue deep into her. Whatever was keeping her body from releasing the building pleasure wave from cresting also preventing it from retreating from the pain.

"Tsk. I should have made you a dog, but no, her Eminence insists on cats. Training is always so much more involved with cats. This is the price of being what you are. Every Fey serves a master."

"I-I-I never agreed!" Jacqueline fought to squeeze out the words between breaths. Jasper's tongue was twisting around in a frenzy of impossible movement inside her while the collar was attempting to freeze her heart solid. Individually, both the pain and pleasure would have been too much to bear, but with both pressing against her mind, each prevented the other from overwhelming her.

"But you will, my dear pet. Make it easy on yourself. Call me Master." Menzo reached around her chest and start to tease her top nipples. "Ask me to finish you off again. This must be soooo agonizing for you." Jacqueline writhed from his touch as he squeezed her dark nipples between his thumb and forefinger. Both the expanding pleasure and pain within her seemed to echo with his words, promising sweet release if only she'd obey.

She felt her lips begin to move without her will. "Please! Ma-" She roared to cut off her traitorous voice as she felt herself slipping. The pressure between the two extremes-- hot and cold, pleasure and pain-- was too much. They would crush her soon. She cast about, searching for something, anything, to save herself. A rock or a branch, but nothing lay within her reach. A bolt of pleasure slammed through her forcing her eyes shut. There in the dark of her eyelids, an entirely different space opened before her. The link to Dave shone before her. She could feel him, and love and worry flowed from it like a jungle waterfall. Thinking of nothing else, she reached out for it, her arm tingling as it ripped away from her flesh and plunged into the link. She felt her hand close around his and he pulled. There was an odd sideways sensation as the pressure of Menzo's two-pronged attack vanished.

Warmth filled her. Not the warmth of Jasper's impossible pleasure, but the comforting warmth of a life-giving campfire. Opening her eyes, she found herself standing in the village before a blazing bonfire, Dave's hand in hers through the link, nothing more than his hand would fit through it.

Within the fire, the rapt faces of the audience from the night of her transformation flowed into each other, flickering as part of the flame. This was what Menzo was truly after; she could feel his desire for it. All the magic he had gathered from the audience, their awe and wonderment. Their belief had made Menzo's glamour real. When Menzo had taken her humanity, mistaking it for what gave her free will, this fire had surged into the gap, becoming part of her very soul. She closed her eyes and stepped into the fire.

The fire was hers; its warm was comforting as she gathered it around herself. Distantly she was aware of Menzo and Jasper alternately teasing and torturing her body, desperately trying to force her obedience. Looking down through the ground of this protected realm she could see her body.

Jacqueline was amazed to see that she was still standing, hanging onto Jasper head while arcing backward as far as her arms would allow. Jasper's muzzle was buried deep between her legs as he continued his rhythmic licking and Jacqueline drove her hips into him with each, individual stroke. The thrusting shook her entire body, making all six of her swollen breasts bounce in unison. Her jaw hung open, tongue lolling out to the side, her lips would have formed an 'O' if they had been anywhere close to each other. Behind her knelt Menzo, his face twisted in concentration as he clawed at her third pair of nipples.

All three of them were flooded with magic. Each stroke of

Jasper's tongue drove more of his pulsing, red, sexual energy into her. It flooded every crevice of her body, clinging to her, preventing the massive orgasm that had built up in her, washing away everything else. But Jasper's own glow was fading, tiring, she could see that even his glamour had begun to fade. Inside the outline of the impossibly attractive leopard was a nearly skeletal man with a cat-like tail and hands with very long fingers.

While Jasper was fire, Menzo was ice. His frozen blue aura poured into her through the collar around her neck, tendrils of ice creeping towards her heart, but being held back by Jasper's own fire. In frustration Menzo would send a spike out from a tendril and it would briefly impale her heart, making it skip a beat before the fire of pleasure melted it away. Menzo himself was the same as the collars around Jasper and her own neck. They were forged of his own being, pieces of him.

Jacqueline felt the pull of her body; this bubble of safety floated on the intersection of pain and pleasure would only preserve her while they were in balance. The red magic flared, its grip already beginning to slip on her. The collar had to be removed before the orgasm crested, or she'd be at Menzo's mercy and unable to withstand the pain. Jacqueline thought furiously, trying to come up with a plan but a tiny orgasm cracked the ground beneath her and she fell back into her body with a cry.

Menzo was whispering in her ear. "That's just a taste of this, Jacqueline. Just ask me for permission and you will come, the pain will stop." His voice was tense and he spoke through gritted teeth.

"Liar." Jacqueline mouthed the word as another crack in Jasper's dam cannoned through her body. Despite it all, she could feel the heat of her bonfire and the sensation of Dave's hand in her own. Menzo seemed unaware of her connection to a different plane, and she had to use that. If this was going to work, she had to act fast.

Closing her eyes, Jacqueline did her best to ignore the writhing of Jasper's tongue and cloak herself in her fire as she focused on Dave. She felt his worry, his urgency to know what was wrong. She squeezed his mental hand in reassurance, and then forced her own fire-coated presence through the link. She fumbled around inside of him for a moment and found the cold thing she was searching for. She sent a wave of apology for the intrusion as she ripped it out with a flaming thought. It was cold, slick and wriggled desperately in her gasp. Pulling it into herself, it spurted out the impact of her anger from last night. For an instant, she was Dave as she attacked him. As he was slammed into the floor, pinned down and laid helpless by the woman he loved; convinced that he would die, devoured by a creature he loved. Jacqueline screamed in horror and ripped the memory away from herself. She had no time to process her emotions as the wave of pleasure slammed to into her like an earthquake mated to a tidal wave.

"NO! NOT YET!" Jacqueline screamed as she thrashed in Menzo's grip, desperately trying to hold off her climax. Her toes' claws bit deep in to the ground as she clamped her interior walls down on Jasper's tongue, trying to still its motion. Her teeth chattered with effort, but she managed to stop herself, her entire body trembling on the very edge. Desperately, she wove the flames of her fire around herself, encasing her entire body in a magical cocoon, trapping the orgasm inside her. It covered everything but the palms of her hands.

"What are you doing, my naughty pet? That won't protect you from me. Come and let's try a new game," Menzo spoke as Jacqueline felt one of his hands threading his fingers through the fur on her belly. She could feel its destination was her throbbing clit. It was relatively unstimulated at the moment, Jasper's tongue was focused on things deep within her. When he touched it, she'd be done.

Desperate to buy a little more time she began to mouth the word he wanted to hear. "M-M-M," her lips chattered and his hand paused for just moment as he grinned. Jacqueline used that moment to gather up all the little shards of glamour littering her mind. She pressed them into the fear, studding its surface with mind-ripping spikes. They bit into her own being as she forced the fear into her hands. The pain made her hiss.

Menzo frowned and shook his head. "You want to say it. You will call me master as you come." Jacqueline felt the compulsion flow from the collar as his reached downward and pressed a dainty finger into her waiting clit. But it was slower than the words that flowed from Jacqueline's mouth.

"MENZO YOU CAN SUCK IT!" She roared and clapped her hands around his very surprised head as the tsunami crashed through her. It triggered a series of supernovas exploding along her spine, and as it reached her skull, the world went white. For a moment, she disappeared into the bliss.

She might have been there for less than a second, or it could have been a year. Slowly, two voices intruded upon that perfect feeling, their harmony drilling through her consciousness. One screamed with pleasure, the other with pain. Her eyes opened to find Menzo looking down on her, his mouth open in a scream of pure terror, while her own scream of pleasure matched his. It was working! The fear had smashed through his defenses, and like the gunpowder behind a bullet, the force of the orgasm had driven the fear deep into the Fey.

Jacqueline's body shuddered. Jasper was still licking her! The laps were slow and unhurried, like a kitten rather than a lion. Each slow lick sent an aftershock rolling through her body. Jacqueline longed to push him away; her body flagged with exhaustion and ached for respite. That was not an option, for her hands remained clamped on the sides of Menzo head. His mouth still hung open in a delicious scream, and each orgasm that Jasper triggered hammered the fear deeper into the Fey. Jacqueline grinned at him watching his eyes widen further with each blow. They were changing, the irises expanding over the whites of his eyes.

The scream cut off with a choking cough, and when it opened again an animal bleat fell from his mouth. Jacqueline could feel his fear now, bleeding into her from the collar around her neck. His thoughts were full of images of her teeth and claws, imaginings of the pain of his neck bitten through by those fangs. Coating those emotions and images with her personal fire, Jacqueline fed them back into him as she pulled him closer. Then she ROARED directly into his face, showing him his fear close up. Whatever sliver of control he had left snapped. "NO!" He bleated and started to thrash in Jacqueline's grip.

With a predator growl Jacqueline kicked Jasper away and sunk her claws into Menzo head. The resulting squeal was utterly delicious as she pulled the bucking Fey closer, trying to get a taste of that elegant neck. He fought her without any sense of beauty or elegance, only the sheer strength of animal panic. Only grunts and bleats escaped his lips as his face started to distort, mouth surging forward into a very pointed muzzle, while black horns erupted from his forehead. He clawed at Jacqueline's paw-hands with his fingers even as they began to stretch and deform. His entire body slimmed, becoming sleek and fragile. He finally broke eye contact with Jacqueline as his eyes moved to the sides of his head, still blue but becoming dark. Unable to pry her paws from his head, he shifted to pummeling her with now sharp, tiny hooves. He struck her nose and Jacqueline released him with her own snarl of pain. He stumbled backwards and tumbled over a tree trunk. Still changing, Menzo's torso barreled, while tan, black and white markings spread over his body as his horns continued to extend. His clothes dissolved into wisps of glamour.

Jacqueline rolled over to watch Menzo becoming increasingly tasty-looking springbuck. She grinned as he blindly struggled to regain control of his body and get away. His legs spasmed unevenly and slammed him into another tree. A short white tail sprouted and immediately flashed warning to everyone around. PREDATOR! He bleated and bayed as his back hooves finally hardened and found purchase on the forest floor. Jacqueline tried to rise, but her exhausted body utterly refused to move. Menzo paused, now completely unrecognizable, except for a splash of blue in the eyes that flashed back at Jacqueline for the briefest of moments before he dashed off into the forest in an erratic, bouncing path.

As soon as the sounds of his hooves striking the earth faded away, Jacqueline let her head fall to the ground. All she could do was lie there and breathe. Jasper had disappeared at some point, but she wasn't really sure how or when he got away. When she had recovered a little strength, she reached up and grabbed the collar around her neck. It snapped off her neck without any resistance, seemingly relieved to be off her neck. Fear radiated from it. Jacqueline tossed it to the side.

She found herself laughing a shallow, breathy laugh of exhaustion. Tears swelled in her eyes. She'd survived again. Not only won but beaten the little bastard without any help. Well, Dave helped a little. Menzo wouldn't be back anytime soon. Hell, she doubted the Fey was even capable of rational thought at the moment. That thought started her purring, reducing Menzo to a docile animal was a sweet irony that she savored.

CHAPTER 12

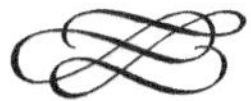

FRIENDS

DAVE STARED AT THE SKY. IT WAS BLUE. WHY WAS IT IN FRONT OF him though? He shifted and discovered that he was lying on his back, although he did not remember laying down. In fact, the last thing he remembered was walking-- no, running-- down the path. He had been running towards...towards…

Jacqueline.

The name, the thought, drove him bolt upright. Jacq, she was in trouble. Something had happened to his wife. Images of spots, the sensation of soft fur under his fingers and her thick, sweet scent rolled through his mind. There was also something else there. The flash of teeth, angry eyes, memories of her violence struggled to be heard, but they were only images now. The heart-hammering fear that had come with them was gone. She had taken it. He could feel the hole, he remembered now.

He had been walking toward her, running whenever his breath caught up with him. Then she was there, inside his head, her sudden presence making him stumble. She was in both pain and ecstasy at once, and she brought them with her. Dave had screamed from the pain and grabbed at his crotch as he fell from the path. She had wanted him, needed something, and although no words had been spoken, he had given it.

Only Fey could do something like that, take a piece of you. Dave shivered as he mentally poked the memories that had made his heart pound from a slight flash of them, now stripped of any emotion, they were just images. That scared him, and this new sense of dread seemed to pool in the hole. Jacqueline was no animal, she was Fey, but that was worse. Would this just be the start? Was she going to eat him from the inside out, bit by bit? Why did she need his fear of her? Did she want him not to be afraid of her?

No. She had needed it for something else. Something had been hurting her. He reached out to her, trying to touch her in the way she had touched him, but the link did not open. He could feel her in the same direction she had been. She was focused on something. Dave ached to know more, but the link didn't give up any more details.

Grumbling, Dave pulled himself out the bushes, zipped up his fly and resumed his trek towards her. It was not until he had almost reached the parking lot and saw that her car was no longer sitting there. Had she gone home? Grinning, he checked his cell phone and then scowled at the blank screen. He pressed the power button, but nothing happened. Dead. Stupid thing. Damn thing was always running out of juice the moment he needed to make a call. Still swearing at his phone, he got into his car and tore out of the parking lot and headed home at a pace more than slightly above the posted speed limits.

His heart jumped with hope as he arrived home. He saw Jacqueline's car sitting in its space, a bit crookedly parked. A grin was spreading over his worried face when he noticed something that stopped it cold. Red was smeared all the over the lip of the trunk and the driver's side door handle. Blood, dried blood, paw prints and messy streaks. Dave's stomach plummeted down the well and he fought to stay on his feet. Blood had never been his forte, and now… That dread reached up from the well his stomach had fallen into and wrapped around his heart. What had Jacqueline done? Had she hurt someone? What if she had? New fear filled him. Maybe she'd never hurt him, but what about others? Was she a man eater? No. He tried to fight off the thoughts. She was better than that. He hoped.

The three flights of stairs had never been so long. His feet felt as heavy as if he was wearing boots constructed from cold iron. His stomach gave a lurch as he looked at the door to their apartment. There was a stain of something on the wood in the hallway. Through the door wafted the whine of an electric guitar, followed by heavy drums… Queen. Dave checked to see if there was anyone watching him with a video camera as this was beginning to feel as if he had walked into a bad horror movie.

He shook himself. That was silly. Jacqueline wouldn't have killed anyone. It could be her blood. What if she was hurt? What then? She could be in there dying and as he waited outside!

That could be true, but Dave had a strong feeling that he wasn't going like what was on the other side of the door, even as he turned the handle.

The smell hit his nose even before the door was fully open. The air in the apartment was thick with the metallic tang of blood, mixed with an acrid scent that that made the bile rise in the back of his throat.

The apartment was dim, all the shades were still drawn, and things were still scattered about from Jacqueline's earlier rampage. There was a light coming from the kitchen doorway, and over the sound of the blaring radio came a soft thwack.

"Jacqueline?" Dave had meant to call out with a loud voice, but it barely registered above a whisper and died away in the face of the music. Holding on to his stomach in a vain hope that his hand might somehow help keep a lid on its contents, he entered the room. "Jacqueline?" He called a little louder now, but the only answer was two more soft thwacks.

Dave bit his lip for a moment, then crossed the room and peered into the kitchen with trepidation. His eyes widened as his eyes caught the glint of bloodstained metal from the butcher's cleaver as Jacqueline brought it down onto a mutilated carcass, severing several ribs from the vertebrae they were attached to.

The kitchen was littered with body parts; all skinned, and on the table was a blue tarp with a huge pile internal organs and a naked deer's head which seemed to watch Dave with a permanent expression of surprise. At the counter where Jacqueline was working, the deer's four legs had been skinned, chopped and stacked. Next to her cutting board was her laptop, its screen marred by a few errant splatters, and a bloody plastic bag covering the mouse. Knifes of countless sizes and shapes were scattered about, tossed aside when they were found lacking.

And Jacqueline… Her fur was caked with dried blood; it stained the light fur of her chest, muzzle and most of her arms a rusty red. She did not notice Dave as she worked to separate the rest of the ribs from the spine, her tail lashing with each fall of the cleaver. She was having fun! His vegetarian wife bared her teeth at the meat as the rib meat fell away from the spine and her white fangs shined in the light.

Dave's brain just stopped as one of her ears oriented on him and then her head swiveled towards him, bringing those teeth to bare. Looking at them, the meat, her joyously gore-covered body, the smell of the blood and bile, it was all too much. All vestiges of his wife had disappeared, replaced with this monster in their kitchen.

She just grinned that predatory grin at him. "Hi, Dave. Do you want to help me with," her tongue curled out of her mouth and ran up the side of her blood spatter muzzle, "dinner?"

It was the last straw for Dave's brain as it conjured an image of his own head sitting on that table. He screamed like wounded animal and bolted.

"DAVE!" Her voice followed him as he rushed for the door. "Dave, I'm sorry!" she shouted again, accompanied by the sound of her claws scrabbling over the tile floor as he vaulted the couch. Had to get away! His hand was closing around the doorknob just as she hit him like a bloody sack of potatoes. Dave thrashed like a panicked animal, sure there was nothing left of her now. She was going to drink his soul and then butcher his body.

But she didn't. Jacqueline wrapped her arms around him and refused to let go. No claws bit into his flesh, no teeth closed around his trachea. "Dave, please calm down. I didn't mean to scare you. I'm sorry, and I love you."

Dave did his best to break free, to push her off of him, and he continued fight even as the panic began to ebb. She was just so goddamned strong, he wanted to win this struggle, even after realized he didn't need to. She wasn't going to kill him, and her soft lips that brushed the back of his neck told him that this blood-soaked, two-hundred-pound predator loved him. Still, Dave fought her if only for pride's sake. He kicked against the door, strained against her arms and tried to pry apart her hands. Nothing worked and he finally sagged against his monstrous wife, tears welling up in his eyes. Too weak. He was too weak. He felt a roughness on the back of his neck as she began to groom the back of his head. It wasn't an unpleasant sensation; he could feel the tenderness of the gesture, even if a small part of him screamed at the inhumanness of it. This was wrong, he should be the stronger one, Dave was the protector of this family. Dave tried not to hate himself as he leaned into Jacqueline's administrations and muttered, "I'm sorry." That little piece of him was just going to have to cope with the fact that things were different now. He still fought back the sob, but this time he lost and shuddered in his lover's arms, ashamed of his doubt. "I'm sorry, Jacq."

"It's okay. I forgot what I must look like at the moment. I thought I was being funny. I didn't mean to scare you, well, this badly. That was mean." She held him for a long time and let Dave regain his composure before she spoke again. "I broke the spell."

"What?" Dave's heart fluttered and his eyes flew open. He rolled away from her so he could look her into her eyes. They were still the expressive, bright amber eyes of a beast, far too large for a human and bearing no visible white. If eyes were truly windows to the soul, then nothing had changed. There was nothing anymore human about her than when he saw her last.

She looked away from his eyes and squeezed Dave's hand. He could feel the granules of blood in her fur press against his skin. It made his stomach flop around like a fish on the dock. "Dave," she whispered, the tone alone killed the fish as memories of high school and college dumpings flooded his mind. "I'm back, I remember how I was and how we were. I was attacked again today."

Dave's eyes went wide and he made to interject but she placed a thick finger over his lips and the word on them died.

"I drove him off. For good, I think. But before I did, I had to make a choice." She looked up at him; those haunting eyes shimmered with wet. "I chose this, Dave. Even after I broke the glamour, he offered me my old self back and I couldn't take it. Just the idea of losing my spots, revolted me. I fought him for them, David. I risked becoming his slave for them."

Dave's face went pale has the realization sunk in. "Is being human that bad?"

Jacqueline looked down again, staring at the four shapely mounds on her chest. "It would be like chewing off my own leg." Both her hands clutched one of Dave's and squeezed it very tightly. "I love you, Dave, but… Things are not going to go back to how things were. This is me now."

"Take me or leave me." Dave's brain finished the sentiment. He swallowed, his mouth as dry as a desert. She liked this? He looked over her gore-splattered features, the tail that curled around her kneeling legs, its tip twitching, the barest trace of her old self swallowed by her feline face. It was one thing to think of this as a disease, that a terrible evil that forced this form upon her. It was another to say that he was married to a monster and he loved her despite imagining himself on the butcher block every time she brought a kill home. It wasn't fair. Dave wanted the old Jacqueline back, the slightly submissive woman who hated her job and was a little obsessed with magic. She was easy to love, and it was easy to get his way. Now this new Jacqueline, beautiful as she was, would be hard to love. He'd be the weak one, and new roles between them would have to evolve.

"Dave?"

"I'm here, hon. I love you." He didn't look at her when he said it. He meant it, but his wheels were still spinning in his head. Calculating.

"You need a drink?"

"Drink?" He looked up at her then, coming out of his storm of thoughts.

She gave his hand another squeeze. "Why don't you change your shirt and go down to the bar for an hour or two while I finish in the kitchen and clean up. I'll buzz ya when the place won't make you vomit. Then we can talk about stuff."

Dave sighed and wiped his eyes. "Alright, Jacq. I can do that." A beer or two or three would indeed make this better.

She gave him a quick lick on the cheek. "No shots, we can't talk if I have to come pick you up. Alright?"

"Yeah."

"I love you, too." And with that, she padded back towards the kitchen to finish her butchery.

Dave could only stare at his wife's spotted tail as she walked away with a confident stride. After she disappeared through the door to the kitchen, he stared at it for a long while.

Confusion ruled his brain as he struggled to his feet and went to the door. He paused before turning the knob and looked back at the kitchen door, the soft sound of butcher's knife again flowing into the apartment. He sighed and opened the door. "We need to talk." The words echoed around his head like an inmate in a rubber room as he exited the building and slipped into the afternoon air. They made him feel like it was high school all over again. Still he could not deny that they had quite a bit of sorting out to do. The soul link, new rules, the fact that they need to move, how she was bloody terrifying to name just a few. He wondered what had happened to Jacqueline in that forest. Dave had seen no confusion in her eyes. No clashing between the old and new Jacqueline. The woman in their kitchen was the outcome of his "therapy." Maybe Dr. Niddler could have salvaged more of Jacqueline's original personality, or perhaps six months of therapy would have ended in the same result. Either way, this was a bed he would have to get used to laying in.

Fortunately, he could sleep anywhere with a few beers in him. The thought made him chuckle as he walked up to the local watering hole, The Winged Pig. It was still well before five o'clock and the bar was sparsely populated when he opened the door. The bartender, Sam, smiled invitingly when Dave slid into a seat at the bar. He'd been here way too often the past two weeks, stopping here on his way back from the hospital.

"Your here a bit early, Dave. What you need?"

Dave laughed inwardly and then sighed. "From you Sam? Just a beer. A very cold beer."

"That I can do." He smiled patiently as he poured the beer and set it in front of Dave. Most of the town knew something had happened to Jacqueline. Even those who were with her on the night she ran into the Fey were fuzzy on the details. The doctors told him this was due to the fact that their experiences of the night were twisted to fuel the magic. Large magics, such as the one that got Jacqueline, often caused memory loss for 24 hours before the incident. "Batteries," as the MDA called them, were often disoriented for days. Sam had listened to Dave's incoherent babbling a couple nights ago while he was trying to decide whether or not to pull Jacqueline out of the hospital. "How's it going? She's home?"

Dave took a long swig of his beer before answering. "Yeah, she's home. It's… been a rough day. It worked, Sam."

"That great! So… why are you here?"

Dave swallowed and looked into his beer, wondering where half of it had gone. Why was he here? Because, despite the therapy, Jacqueline was having a blast while covered head-to-tail in deer gore and he just couldn't handle it. So she was finishing up butchering her kill, and he was waiting down here like a wimp. He emptied his glass. "It's…" He tried to tell Sam about how it felt to have the entire dynamic of his relationship suddenly turned upside down. The fur, the tail, the inhuman mannerisms: those were big changes, but it was finding himself on the bottom in their relationship that really had him weirded out. It was a tough thing to admit that Jacqueline's strength had him frightened. He had always been in the driver's seat of the relationship. They had followed his career to this town, where Jacqueline had only been able to find a job that she detested. Now she "owned" him. Claimed him like a true Fey would, and he had let her in the heat of passion. And he had a feeling that even with her head clear, Jacqueline's new dominance was not something that she was even be capable of curbing. She was a predator, and the balance of their equation had shifted. Now he was the delicate one, the one that paled at the disgusting jobs. He felt weak and effeminate around her. Hell, he had been the one crying just a little while ago hadn't he?

Could he live like this? That was the question, wasn't it? He loved her and she clearly loved him, but was that enough? Could they both be happy with her as she was?

He found his voice at the bottom of his beer. "I'm the one on the bottom now. I'm always going to be on the bottom from now on." He looked up to Sam, but found that he was gone, moved on to other customers while he was thinking. Nobody seemed to have heard him, which was good in retrospect. He motioned to Sam for another beer. He was probably going to be a little sloppy when he headed back, but he'd need all the courage in the bar to admit to Jacqueline how she was making him feel.

Five beers later, the world had started to blur, but that magical courage was nowhere to be found. He would have kept looking for it, but a small voice interrupted him, "Hey hey, big guy!"

Dave turned toward the voice and blinked when he found a very strange looking man on the stool next to him. He was short, painfully thin and had two long black horns with a subtle curve protruding from his forehead. His slender face had a black nose with large, deer-like ears jutting from the side of his head. Thin, tan fur covered his skin. However the strangest part of him were his eyes-- they seemed several sizes to large for his sockets, there were no whites at all, and he had huge pupils rimmed with a brilliant blue iris. They never met Dave's gaze, instead darting around the room as if he expected something to jump out of the shadows and grab him. Dave's mouth worked for a moment, searching for words that seemed to have slipped off his tongue. He took a gulp of his beer, moistening his mouth, and tried again. "Who are you?"

He tittered, "Just somebody who has an idea of what you're going through." He tapped his antlers as he spoke. "You might say that I used to be much farther up the food chain," he laughed, a coughing bleat.

Dave felt himself sway as he examined the little man. "Soooo," he slurred, "You were humaaan, just like my wife?" Mentally, he cursed his stupid drunken tongue. "She's a big cat now."

As the 'c' word left Dave's lips, the little man shivered and his large ears flicked. He recovered quickly, but his little two fingered hands trembled. He gave Dave a little smile that gave the distinct impression that the little man was a moment away from bolting. "Well, I wouldn't compare myself to your wife exactly. I hope my condition is far less, permanent."

Dave nodded sagely, interested in the little man. "So, its not a re-recusif, recursive glamour? They can fix it?"

"In time, I shall be my old self again. But in the meantime, it's bit difficult. I'm not used to being small and," the antelope man winced visibly, "breakable."

Dave looked down at the little guy and felt a twinge of sympathy. He shuddered to imagine what would happen if he came home to Jacqueline looking like this guy. Jacq would just eat him; he even had little hooves for feet. "I hope your wife is gentle." Dave's eyes widened as that phrase left his mouth and then winced. "Sorry." He quickly turned back to his beer.

But the little man didn't scamper away, instead he started to giggle, a sharp sound that made the back of Dave's neck prickle. Dave risked a glance back at the antelope man. He clutched at the bar with his dainty two fingered hands, their knuckles whitening as his entire body shook with effort as the giggles were tortured into hissing noises escaping between his teeth.

Dave stared at his companion, "Hey, you okay?" He reached out and poked the man's coarsely furred shoulder. The stranger exploded into a bleating laughter, throwing his long neck back and tipping his face to the ceiling as the inhuman laugher erupted like a volcano. "BLEEEH! BLEEEH! BLEEEH!" Recoiling, Dave very nearly knocked himself off the stool. The animal-like laughter filled the small bar. The patrons of the bar had begun to notice the stranger blinking at him as if waking from a deep sleep. Dave realized for the first time that the antelope man wasn't wearing a scrap of cloth on his body.

"BLEEEEH! BLEEH! Bleeeh!"

Just as Dave was about to slide off his stool and slip away, the laughter faded and the man's head fell to bar with an audible clunk that made Dave wince. Amazingly, all the other patrons immediately turned away from the spectacle, leaving Dave alone with the little antelope man slumped on the bar. Something that damn MDA man had said echoed back through Dave mind, "Magic is going to wrap itself around everything around her, including you, your family and your neighbors." Dave's head felt remarkably clear now and he cast a glance at the other pub patrons. Had he been like that until recently? Unwilling to see the magical unless it was shoved in his face, would he have just turned back around like everyone else three weeks ago? Maybe leaving would be the smart thing. The little guy was clearly a bit unbalanced, and he did have his own problems to deal with. But Jacqueline would understand him having to help the guy out, right? Of course she would. Swallowing, he leaned over to look at the stranger, who was still laughing, though quietly now, a thin smirk at the corner of his muzzle. "Hey," Dave began, "you okay?"

He snorted and flicked his long ears. "Heh yeeeaah. That was funny."

"What was funny?"

"My old lady. She's not gentle."

"Oh. I thought you said you were getting better?"

The little man grinned sheepishly as he sat back up on the barstool and focused the bright blue eyes directly on Dave's, "Oh, I am. I've got the hands back now, but there's not enough time any more."

Dave found himself looking right into the little man's eyes, there was something off about them. It wasn't that they were inhuman like the rest of him, but he couldn't quite find the proper word for them. Mentally, Dave shook himself and turned back to the stranger's conversation, "Time for what?"

"To complete my task, I mean, my job. I have a very, very," the small hoof hands began to tremble as he spoke, his voice fading to a bare whisper, "literal deadline. There's not enough time!" His eyes grew wide and, near panicked, exposed an ocean of white. Dave could not help but feel his heart squirm in sympathy for the little man.

"W-what did you have to do?" Dave asked, a note of confusion in his voice, it wasn't really his business, but the man plain needed someone to talk to. No harm in listening to the man.

"It had been a simple request. Just a trivial hunt, you see, but I wanted to impress her. Show her that I was the greatest of her admirers. You understand that, don't you? You give valuable gifts to those important to you, right?"

Dave nodded, thinking of the silver circlet around Jacqueline's tail. He could almost see it in the blue-rimmed black of the little man's eyes.

"I crafted a brilliant gem for my lady, full of the fire of will. But it burned me! Can you believe the audacity of burning your own creator! Like a child spitting in its mother's eye! I hunted it, fought fair and square, but it bested me! Warped me into this trembling thing you see before you. I cannot bear her presence anymore!" With each word, the man's eyes seem to loom larger in Dave's vision. There was nothing in the world but those terrified eyes; he couldn't bear the sight of them looking so hurt, so vulnerable. His little hands clutched at one of Dave's hands with a desperate strength. "Will you help me?"

Thoughts were suddenly hard for Dave to form, lost within the depths of those eyes, but he pushed through the fog. "Wha-what do you need me to do?" It was as if the five beers had snuck up and sapped him from behind.

"I need someone to hunt for me. I can't do it myself, not in time."

"Hunt?"

"Yeesss. You're a strong man, stronger than she thinks you are. I can help you be top dog again. You want that, don't you? Make things simple again."

Dave heart leapt in hope. Simple would be better, the way things were supposed to be. "Yeah."

"Good boy. Now slip this around your neck."

CHAPTER 13

THE MONSTER IN THE MIRROR

JACQUELINE STARED AT HER SLIGHTLY SOGGY REFLECTION. IT WAS the first time she had actually looked at herself since she had shaken that ridiculous notion that she had been born this way. She had to admire the magic's craftsmanship-- the way that her head was indeed that of the animal she resembled, but with the features altered just enough to give her human-like expressions. The thick black lips at the tip of her muzzle, combined with the corners of her muzzle gave her the ability to frown or smile. Her eyes, while lacking any sort of white, were large and expressive. Combined with how she positioned her ears, she could nearly mimic any human expression, although she looked quite threatening when she grinned. The fangs in her mouth had a very different quality than human teeth. She traced her thick fingers down the length of her muzzle and reveled in the sensation of her hand bending her sensitive whiskers. Something she couldn't have felt before Menzo did this to her.

Guilt trickled through her for enjoying it so much. It had been a terrible, evil thing for Menzo to do. She would have spent the rest of her life chained in a cage as a plaything for the Fey Court if he had succeeded in kidnapping her. Yet, despite that, she reveled to find herself in this body; she had never liked her old one. It had always been a struggle to maintain it, and she always dreamed of becoming something else. Partially "the grass is always greener" she was sure. Being a cat would probably come with all sorts of minor annoyances. She frowned down at her six swollen breasts. She cupped one, feeling its weight in her paw and felt the need blossom within her. Sucking in breath she removed her paw and gripped the sink in front of her, waiting for the sensation to fade away.

Annoyances such as being in heat and perhaps back pain. Menzo's little trick had not faded. Even though Jasper's scent was finally out of her fur, the heat he had awakened remained deep inside her. It wasn't overwhelming, but it was like standing on a cliff- - a step in the wrong direction and it was all down hill. She had allowed herself some exploration while she showered, but it had done nothing to relieve it. The need was far deeper than she could reach with her short fingers.

She smiled at her reflection and struck a pose. Hands on hips, chest out, tail lashing and a sultry expression. "I am a sexy beast." She told herself. It was true, even if her facial expression looked a bit more hungry than sultry. But Dave needed a wife more than he needed the monster at the moment, and her gaze shifted from her mirror to her closet and sighed. Tonight she needed to show her husband that the old Jacqueline was still there for him. For him, she would see how human she could get.

In the back of her closet, there were a few dresses that had escaped yesterday's rampage, a range of sizes that she kept just in case. After wrapping her torso with ace bandages to compress her extra assets, she found a simple and sleeveless red dress that fit her. Its long skirt hid her oddly shaped legs and tail. The bodice and bra emphasized her top set of breasts and made her middle set almost disappear. It was odd that the dress fit so perfectly, it had never fit to her satisfaction before. Now she wondered if she had somehow bought it for her future self.

She styled her short brown hair into something approaching her old hairstyle, waves of brown encircling her face. Now that just left this face of hers, and she pawed through the cosmetics looking for something that might help. False lashes? She considered it and then rejected the idea on the basis that it would look like she was trying way too hard. In the end, the only thing she used was a bit of lipstick, making her black lips an almost human shade of red.

Checking herself in the mirror, she looked good, civilized. A bit formal for just a heart-to-heart, but she wanted to show Dave that she could be the old Jacqueline sometimes too. It wasn't particularly comfortable, the compression of her breasts was causing an ache that resonated with her deeper needs. She was very careful to keep her hands away from any tender bits as she lowered herself onto the couch. If something happened tonight with Dave, it would happen. They needed to talk first. Unless he came home drunk, then she might be entitled to dole out a little "punishment." The thought made her lick her chops hungrily as she turned on the TV to wait for her sweet morsel to come home to her.

A boring sitcom later, he still hadn't shown up. Jacqueline's ears roamed like confused radar dishes, several times they locked on to the sound of heavy footsteps in the stairway but each time they passed by their apartment door. It had been over two hours since she had sent Dave to the bar. Where was he? The question sounded stupid in her own head.

Dave was busy getting drunk at the bar where she had sent him. With a rumbling sigh, she stood and went to the kitchen. Her cell phone sat in its charger, a tiny little flip phone that was half a decade out of date. She gave it an accusing glare before she grabbed it with her clumsy hands. Holding it proved simple enough, but the tiny keys were bit a more of a problem. Her fingers were too large to hit a single key and her claws slid across the smooth metal keys and into depths between. Ironically, it was the claw she had fractured back at the hospital that proved to be the easiest to prod the electronic device and call Dave's cell phone. However that bit of obedience didn't stop Jacqueline from hurling the phone across the room when her call went straight to voice mail.

Jacqueline huffed, she had no idea what the phone number of the bar was. If her luck held, Dave might be too drunk to find his way home. Maybe he'd try to run away again. She'd just have to hunt him down then.

Once she was outside the apartment, walking towards the stairway, it occurred to Jacqueline that perhaps hunting down Dave like a wounded elk wasn't the most rational course of action. The civilized course would have been to Google the bar's phone number and inquire after her husband's state of inebriation, but her feet did not change course. She pounded down the stairs as fast as her tight dress would allow. There was a growing urge to drop to all fours and run, as with each step the sense of dread grew.

A teenage kid, his neck draped in fake gold chains, nearly collided with her. They both stopped inches from each other. A lecherous grin grew on his face as he scanned up Jacqueline's form until it passed over her breasts and he saw Jacqueline's face, her fangs exposed in an instinctual snarl. With an incoherent cry, he flung himself to the side of the stairway with a force that made his bling jingle.

There was a mental click within Jacqueline's head that caused her to stare at the kid in horror. He flinched away from her gaze, throwing his hands up to protect himself. "Please, don't eat me."

The sound of his words never entered her head, Jacqueline was focused on something else entirely. "Chains." She felt for the link that she had forged to Dave's soul. It was gone.

Dress be damned, Jacqueline ran. She vaulted over the railing and down the remaining story of the building. She burst from the apartment building on all fours, traveling fast enough that pedestrians would swear they'd been buzzed by a spotted motorbike. She hit the door to the Flying Pig just as her heart threatened to burst. The door rushed inward and banged against the wall with the crack of a gunshot. Everyone in the bar swiveled toward Jacqueline. She could see the whites of the crowd's eyes, but none of them belonged to Dave. He wasn't here. Slowly, Jacqueline realized that she was still on all fours, panting like a husky in Hawai'i, her heart beating so hard that it was making her ears ring.

"What the hell is that?" some in the crowd whispered.

Jacqueline forced herself to stand back on two legs. The bartender started. "Are you Jacqueline?"

She fixed her eyes on him and the unfamiliar man swallowed. It

was too late to do this subtly, so she went for bluntness. "Where is he?" her voice had an edge of a growl to it.

The man sucked in his breath. "He was here a half hour ago. He left you a note." He held up a slip of paper. This was not how Jacqueline had wanted to reintroduce herself to the neighborhood. Nothing for it now. She stalked across the silent bar, feeling the eyes of the crowd on her as they parted to make way for her passage. The muscles in her legs screamed in protest, but she ignored them as well as the crowd as she plucked the letter from the bartender's hand. It wasn't from Dave, she knew that before she opened it. The letter reeked of an entirely different personage. One that made her lips twist in a snarl.

Ignoring the bartender's panicky look, Jacqueline's paws fumbled to open the paper. In her haste, her claws tore holes in it before she finally handed it back to bartender with a growl, "Open it."

His worried eyes blinked once.

Jacqueline huffed and waved the paper under his nose. "Open it, *please!* I don't want to rip it any more!"

Comprehension dawned in the man's eyes. "Oh!" He took the paper back, deftly unfolded it and handed it back to her.

Jacqueline's green eyes roamed over the fine handwriting within the note. Then crumpled it into a tiny wad of paper. She looked up at the Bartender. "Do you have a crowbar I could borrow?

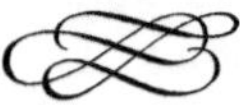

CHAPTER 14

TRICKS AND TRAPS

Even wrapped in a towel and sitting on the seat next to her, Jacqueline could feel the cold iron crowbar as she drove back toward the park. It wasn't hot or cold per se. It was more like a constant tug on her awareness as the metal pulled on the threads of magic around her.

I have something you want, Jacqueline.

The words of the letter were burned into Jacqueline's mind. How could she have let Dave venture off on his own? Why had she simply assumed that she had driven Menzo off? Stupid, stupid, stupid! The word banged around her skull as the gate to the national park loomed into her headlights. Normally, the forests were forbidden after dark, but the bar gate to the parking lot yawned open as her headlights struck the dull green paint. It had been early evening when she had left the bar, but night had pulled the last remnant of sunlight from the sky when her little car rolled through the park gate. The moon shined down on the world, and to Jacqueline's eyes the silver light seemed harsh and glaring, staring down on her like a disapproving aunt.

The car coughed and puttered as Jacqueline pulled into a

parking space, the engine dying on its own before Jacqueline even reached for the key.

"Oh, so it's going to be like that, is it?" Jacqueline muttered as she stared out into the dark of the forest. The shadows of the trees were so deep that they refused to part even for Jacqueline's inhuman eyes. Glaring at them, Jacqueline reached over and wrapped her stubby fingers around the bundled crowbar. She hissed as pain flared in her hand, the gravity of the raw iron clutched her very bones. It shouldn't hurt like this, dammit. Glancing over at the paw, the spots on its fur seemed to tremble. Growling, Jacqueline shut her eyes and focused on herself-- her body, her bones, the way her muscles were strung. No human would know the sensation of claws slipping out of their sheaths and digging into the plastic mat beneath her feet. There was no illusion in that sensation, no idealized world, the dirt that clung to the fur around her footpads pulled uncomfortably at the follicles in her skin. Yes, magic had shaped her body, but a statue is no less real than the stone it is carved from. Jacqueline opened her eyes, the pain of the iron had not subsided, but her spots no longer quivered in fear of the iron.

Careful not to touch the exposed hook of the crowbar she pulled it across her lap and stepped out of the car. A sudden wind screamed through the trees and hit her with such a chilling force that she nearly stumbled. Jacqueline planted her feet and turned into the wind as it pierced her pelt with icy knifes. It parted her fur around her breasts and between her legs, blowing her tail straight out behind her.

Jacqueline thrust the crow bar out in front of her with two hands, the wind whistled over the exposed iron hook at one end of the towel. Lips curling back to show the trees her glistening fangs, Jacqueline roared in challenge to the forest's anger.

"ENOUGH! I will not be driven away! I am here to answer a challenge and I will not be refused!"

The wind continued to howl in her ears as she took a step forward. The wind redoubled, and she could feel it broaden its attack, trying to push her back, the iron crowbar seemed to vibrate from the force. The ache in her own hands lessened as it pulled at the magic driving the very air. She bared her teeth and took another step. The wind fell away as if suddenly exhausted.

The shadows beneath the trees quivered. Then a voice came from the forest, "Take your death metal and be gone. We will not ask again." It took a moment for Jacqueline to parse the words as the syllables were composed of the sounds of the forest, wind over leaves, hoots of an owl and other unlikely sounds all from different parts of the forest, but blended together to make words.

Jacqueline squinted her eyes at the dark. Was this a trick by Menzo or was she actually dealing with the forest itself? Perhaps both. She thought hard, dredging up everything she knew about spirits. "I have no quarrel with you, spirit. My quarry is within, and my iron will not trouble you so long as my hunt is unimpeded."

"You are not of me! Your hunt shall take from me!"

"Neither is my prey!" Jacqueline snarled and took another step, her anger sending her tail lashing behind her. "I seek what is mine! I will have my husband back and will devour the Fey called Menzo!"

The wind hissed back, "You seek those who are under my protection! I will not allow..."

"Bullshit. Nice try, Menzo." Jacqueline skipped forward and swung her crowbar at the darkness beneath the trees. The moving shadow shattered like a windowpane, and a bleat of panic sounded from deep in the forest. The shards of shadow dissolved as moonlight stabbed down through the forest canopy like daggers of light. "Forest spirits in North America don't grant protection to anything that wasn't born within it. Fey don't qualify. Show yourself if you want to deal."

There was no answer, but Jacqueline hadn't actually expected any, already walking deeper into the forest. His fear hung in the air, making her stomach rumble, but it seemed to be everywhere, giving no clue to where the Fey was hiding. Without the glamour of the false forest spirit, pain crept back into her hands as the metal hungered for more magic, it felt like her paws had been plunged into ice water. Still, she didn't dare let it go. With her own bonfire exhausted from this afternoon, the iron was the only thing that would protect her from Menzo's mind-bending magics.

Her eyes scanned the ground as she hurried along the path, looking for any disturbance on the packed earth. If only that whole jungle fantasy had been real, then she'd actually know how to track her quarry instead of fumbling blindly into what had to be a trap. He would spring it just as soon as she dropped the crowbar, and the Fey could probably wait until her fingers snapped off. Tears blurred Jacqueline's vision as she stumbled forward. The iron's grasp was reaching up into her arms now.

Despair raged within her, and she abandoned all pretense of stealth and called out into the forest. "DAVE! DAVE, WHERE ARE YOU!"

"Jacqueline!" A distance voice answered her. Was it real? Did it matter?

Hope burst from her heart, pushing back against the iron's hunger. "DAVE!" She roared in answer to it as she rushed towards the voice.

"JACQ!" It was closer now, she was sure of it. Then he called again. Her legs carried her towards him, and her tail acted as a rudder as she wove between the trees, holding the crowbar under the crook of her arm like a jousting knight. Even the trees bent to avoid her as she charged through.

Jacqueline vaulted a small hedge, bursting out into a clearing. There he was. Standing in the middle of it, hands cupped around his mouth preparing to shout her name once again. Jacqueline's heart surged as he looked up at her with wide eyes. He looked intact and whole. Time seemed to freeze as Jacqueline's heart exploded with hope and joy at the sight of him. Abandoning all pretense of caution, she staked the tip of the crowbar into the earth before closing the remaining distance between them on all fours.

Dave eyes widened further as he watched Jacqueline streak towards him. "Jacq?!" he cried in almost panic right before Jacqueline bowled into him. Hugging him to the ground, she savaged him with kisses, licks and muzzle rubs. She wanted to ask him, berate him and tell him so many things that the words got all jumbled together and came out as a mixture of happy rumbles and clicks. Her arms and hand felt like fire as the feeling exploded back into them, but she ignored it, she ignored everything but Dave as he closed his arms around her, threading his fingers through her fur.

"It's alright, Jacq. I'm okay. Everything's going to be alright."

She so desperately wanted to believe him. With the iron gone from her grasp, she felt alive, like the metal had sucked away all the sensations from her body, but now she felt every follicle as the heat flared between her legs and hardened her nipples. He smelled so good, tasting of salt, but there was something else there too. A faint hint of musk that she had never scented before. She kissed him hard, her muzzle against his lips, her tongue against his, and he pushed back against her eagerly. Something was different. He tasted off.

Tearing herself away from him, Jacqueline grabbed his face with both hand paws and stared deep into his eyes. There were flecks of gold in his dark brown irises. "What did he do to you, Dave? What did you give him?"

Strong hands wrapped around Jacqueline's wrists as a curious look entered his eyes and one corner of his mouth quirked upwards into a smirk. "I didn't have to give him anything, Jacq. He just fixed everything." Jacqueline saw the collar then, a thin gold braid around his neck. "It will be like it was before." Claws sprouted from his fingers as his grip on her wrists grew from strong to crushing.

"Dave! Stop it! Your hurting me!" Jacqueline squeaked in panic.

Dave's voice deepened into a feral growl, "You hurt me. You were going to eat me! Why should I stop?"

"Because I asked you to, and I love you," Jacqueline whispered.

The soft words hit Dave like a punch, and he gasped like he'd been hit in the gut. The grip on Jacqueline's wrists slacked and, seizing the opportunity, she twisted out of his grip. She scrambled backward on all fours.

First looking down at his hands with a surprised expression, Dave blinked dumbly then moved them to meet Jacqueline's worried gaze. The Gold flecks in his eyes had grown to spots. "That's not fair! I was on top! I was winning the game!" he wailed at her.

"Dave, think about this, you are in a forest in the dead of night.

This isn't the time for fantasies. We have to go home." Jacqueline slowly backed away from her husband. She smelled waves of anger rolling off of him as sweat poured from his pores, making steam rise off his bare chest as he struggled to get his feet under himself.

He sneered, showing a mouth of jagged teeth. "Isn't this how you wanted it to be, Jacqueline? In the forest like an animal? Our apartment isn't good enough for you! I wasn't enough for you!" His body began to swell, muscles and bone flowing like water into a larger, more powerful configuration.

"No, please, Dave." Jacqueline kept her head low to the ground and backed away from him, step by step, keeping her muscles coiled like springs should he move to grab her. Her tail lashed behind her, not with anger or fear, but deliberately searching for the crowbar she had planted. In the back of her mind, she could feel it, a little drain on the world, but it felt so far away. "I was still sick. I didn't mean to scare you. To hurt you. I'm sorry."

"YOU CHOSE THIS!" Dave howled at her, his eyes completely consumed by the gold as black, shaggy fur burst from under tearing human skin. "YOU COULD HAVE COME BACK! YOU COULD HAVE BEEN HUMAN AGAIN! NOW I HAVE TO HUNT YOU! I HAVE TO KEEP YOU! YOU! You... ARRGH!" Dave's tirade stopped as the changes reached his face. He buried his face in his hands as a long, black muzzle pushed from out from his mouth, his face stretching like a rubber mask, peeling away from the new bone structure. The skin tore and fell from the wolf's head. The creature that had been Dave was now a massive beast of rippling muscle, easily three times the bulk of the original man. His form was humanish, with long arms like an ape, the fingers capped with talons. The head was not of a noble animal, but dredged from the nightmares of long dead peasants, sporting a massive maw so crammed with jagged teeth that it couldn't close properly. It looked down first at the tatters of Dave's face on the grass, then threw back its head and let loose howl that sounded like the roll of thunder.

Jacqueline knew it was time to run.

CHAPTER 15

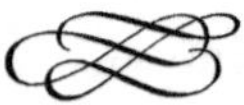

THE HUNT

BEFORE THE HOWL HAD EVEN STARTED TO FADE, JACQUELINE scrabbled for the tree line, the panic overwhelming any other thought. She ran right past the crowbar. It wouldn't help her now. Her claws bit into the earth for traction, her heart pounding in her chest for the second time that night. As the howl faded, she felt his massive paws thunder through the ground. A second howl sliced through the forest, hitting her spine like a bolt of lightning, making every single hair on Jacqueline's body stand straight with fear. Sharp cracks behind her rattled like gunfire as the massive wolfman barreled behind her, not giving pause to any obstacle, just crashing through the forest with the grace of a bulldozer. Jacqueline ran as hard as her legs and arms could carry her, images of those massive jaws crushing her spine filled her head providing the fire to propel her well beyond the point where her muscles' complainants turned to an outraged scream.

Despite her best efforts, the blur of the trees around her began to slow and her tired paws began to miss the ground, making her stumble into the sides of the trees. She chanced a glance behind her. Dave was less than a hundred feet away, loping after her like an angry gorilla, his long black tongue hanging out over rows of teeth, streaming blood and foamy spittle. As his golden eyes caught hers, his pace doubled, charging with an evil grin on his muzzle.

Jacqueline did what any cat would do. With a startled rowl, she booked it to the biggest tree. Her powerful legs launched her onto the thick trunk and she scrambled up the rest of the way with her claws. The tree was ancient, and the trunk almost as wide has Jacqueline's car. She only stopped climbing after the branches started to thin beyond the point they would safely support her weight. A nervous chuckle escaped her lips as she reached the end of the line and the image of a puppy chasing a kitten sprang to her mind. A howl that raked her ears like bones on a chalkboard quickly reminded her that her situation was much less cute.

Dave stared up at her from the forest floor, his golden eyes seemed hollow and dull. Seemingly disconnected from the rest of his body which raged and clawed at the tree. He circled it, howling again. Seeing that he wouldn't or couldn't climb, Jacqueline slumped against the trunk of the tree and took a moment to catch her breath.

"Oh, that's a good boy!"

The sound of THAT voice sent an icy knife through her heart. It was different-- more nasal and even higher pitch that put it in the squeak territory, but there was no doubt as to the voice's owner. "Menzo," Jacqueline growled.

"In the flesh." A small antelope creature walked into view from somewhere below. He stood on two hooves, and to Jacqueline's distress, carried what appeared to be a small bow in his hands with a quiver of arrows strung over his back. He looked up at Jacqueline and grinned. "Maybe in the fur is more accurate?"

Dave quickly trotted over to him and sat down next to the Fey, who scratched him behind the ears, having to stretch to reach it. Dave's tongue lolled happily. Jacqueline hissed at him possessively before she could stop herself. The Fey flinched. "Hands off him, Menzo. Undo to whatever you've done. NOW!"

He gave a nervous bleat but shook himself and planted his little hoof feet. "Ah no. He is mine even more than you are, my p-precocious pet."

"Turn him back, Menzo! Let him go! It's me you want!" Jacqueline felt as if she was reading the script of an over-wrought movie, but she couldn't let Menzo reduce her husband to some sort of pet. There had to be a way to convince him to let Dave go at least.

"Oh ho, I think not, kitty. Dave here is what stands between you and me. Without him to protect me, I couldn't stand to be with the same forest as you. This," he gestured to his tan furred form, "is more than a little inconvenient, but I must thank you for providing me with such an intimate link to your husband."

Jacqueline's eyes bugged as her stomach dropped into her knees "A link?"

The little man grinned; his black horns glimmered in the moon-light with an almost demonic joy. "The Queen would have taught you all of this. How mortal souls constantly seek their reunion. You should thank me, Jacqueline."

"What? Why?" Jacqueline's stomach pitched itself into her feet.

"Care must be taken when harvesting mortal fear. So many nasty things will regrow in a wound like that. Dave here was well on his way to developing serious mental health issues when I found him." Menzo gave Dave an affectionate pat. "He'll be much happier with us, wearing all that envy and fear on the outside. Won't you, boy."

Dave gave a happy wuff. The sound made Jacqueline's own heart tear. This couldn't be. Fear clicked over to hot rage.

"NO!" And before she had even registered a plan, Jacqueline leapt. Launching herself away from the tree with a roar, she dove towards Menzo. The Fey jumped straight up with a surprised bleat as Jacqueline sailed towards him. Inches away from him, she collided with a wall of black fur. No time for reason, thought or mercy, Jacqueline acted. She tore into the foul tasting fur with fangs and claws. A yelp of pain reached her ears and warm blood spat-tered her tongue. She sprung away, slamming her feet into Dave's side to jump away. Dave's jaws closed on the exact place she'd been as he hit the ground sideways. Then she flew, tumbled and landed on all fours, only to spring away again. Instinct was her only guide as she bounded back up another tree, Dave's gnashing teeth inches from her tail.

The scent of pine tickled the roof of her mouth as she landed on the thin trunk as if it were no different from a patch of ground. Muscles coiled and pushed against it before gravity could grab her, arcing herself backwards over the wolf below. Jacqueline's mind had been reduced to a single thought. *Kill Menzo.* That taste of her own husband's blood had seared it into her mind. No peace would be had until nothing remained of the Fey but pixie dust.

Her body understood and obeyed. With a savage twist her body righted itself just in time to see the white of Menzo's tail dancing into the forest. Snarling, Jacqueline hit the ground running, barely feeling the impact jolt up her wrists. She roared, "MENZO!" The Fey bleated and redoubled his effort, springing along on his tiny hooves like a kangaroo. Jacqueline heard the pounding of Dave's paws behind her, beating like a lethal drum. Each beat fueled her hatred of the tiny creature in front of her. He'd taken her husband, twisted him into nothing more than toy.

He had to die.

Her limbs were on fire, but she drove onwards, her claws tearing through the ground beneath her. Menzo glanced back, his too-blue eyes wide with panic. Then there were five of him streaking off in different directions, but Jacqueline ignored the pale imitations, only one carried the fear. The punishing pace of their chase became a beat of a second drum within her mind. Jacqueline gathered the burning pain of her tortured limbs, building it into a bonfire, kindled with the scraps of her remaining humanity. Her spine lengthened, her hair fell away, her breasts withered and her thumbs withdrew, leaving nothing but Jacqueline the beast. Finally, shed of everything nonessential and guided by the beat of the hunt, Jacqueline began to close on her quarry.

She smacked his legs out from under him with a swipe of her paw, sending Menzo into an out of control somersault. Jacqueline leaped over him to avoid entangling herself and felt a sting in her ribs as she passed over. The ground greeted her far too soon and she tasted the pungent grit of the damp soil in her mouth as she slammed onto her side, hot pain exploding into her chest. A giggle reached her ears as her head swam and her limbs pedaled in the air trying to find the ground.

A dark shape moved into her moonlight, and Jacqueline lashed out at it. Swatting desperately at it, her claws found flesh and something yelped in pain. Jacqueline felt a hot, feverish heat spreading through her chest.

"Aw, she scratch you boy? Give her a moment and she'll come around." Menzo's voice was so high-pitched that it was like needles sinking into Jacqueline's ears. She snarled, pushing herself back onto all fours. They wobbled, but held. Dave stood before her, blood dripping from two parallel slashes on his nose. Behind him, she could hear Menzo's mad laughter. Jacqueline tried to growl, but it came out as more as a whine as the heat within her threaded down between her legs. Dave's bestial form didn't look so horrible from this angle, Jacqueline thought as her eyes flowed across his bulging muscles. And there was something noble buried in that oily scent of his.

Jacqueline shook herself. What happened? This wasn't right. Dave was a monstrous thing born of nightmares. She couldn't be attracted to this. She loved him, but not like this. What had Menzo done to her now? She looked under her torso where a broken arrow lay on the ground beneath her, its heart shaped tip shined wetly.

"Just think how great if will feel when he mounts you, Jacqueline." Menzo's head popped from behind the hairy beast before her. "He'll show you how much he loves you, pounding you until there's not another thought in your spotted little head."

To her utter horror, Jacqueline's felt herself dampen at the thought of Dave's, probably, huge cock spearing her insides. The nipples on her stomach prickled with anticipation. Dave whuffed softly, his doggy-like grin growing lecherously as he stepped forward. His smell sank into Jacqueline's head, an oily musk of fear and anger but, oh, so male. Jacqueline's body cried out for it. Surely it wouldn't be so bad. Just to give in this once. He was her husband after all.

Jacqueline screamed and shook her head, pawing at her nose,

trying to get the scent out of it. The glamour clawed at her mind. She had to get it off. Had to break it. The crowbar; that was it. If she could just remember where it was. Jacqueline backpedaled, nearly tripping over her tail. Dave strutted toward her confidently as the feral glamour she had spun around herself began to crack. The need yawned within her as the woman parts of her began to return.

There was nothing to be done but run. She ran! Away from Dave, away from this cursed heat in her body. Dave's howl of excitement tunneled through her ears, down her spine and made her explode with knee buckling NEED. Sending her traitorous body crashing to the ground, her tail arcing into the air. She gasped as the glamour cracked under the strain, her six breasts swelling back into existence. Each tit yearned for his touch. Her ears caught the soft whooshing sound of each of his confident steps behind her. He could have her at any moment. She reached out inside herself for anything she could use, anything at all.

This close, Jacqueline could feel Dave's link. An infected wound in her mind, the passage blocked by oozing pus. Jacqueline threw it away. The burnt out bonfire lay beyond it, sputtering out between the empty jungle huts of the original fantasy that Menzo had fed to her. The flame of pain she had built it with was fizzling, leeching back into her over extended limbs as the humanity she had entrapped it with slunk back into her like a sullen lover. As the flame drew down, her own exhaustion began to smother her like a heavy blanket. The price of her failed hunt. Burning herself to fuel it had been a mistake.

"Someone please help me," Jacqueline pleaded into her own mindscape, into the forest surrounding her as something cold nosed her nether. She cried out loud from the sensation of pure *"fuck me now"* need that rippled through her body. Her tail's tip arced over her back and brushed the top of her head. "Please, Dave. Not like this!" she whimpered. Squeezing her eyes shut, she waited for the pleasure that would finally wash her away. There was nothing left for her to resist with, her body cried out with heat and advertised its desire to be bred like animal.

The wait continued. His hot breath agonized her swollen sex.

She could hear his nostrils sucking in her scent. What was he waiting for?

Jacqueline craned her head around to look behind her. Dave hunched behind her on all fours, broad nose inches from her bared sex. Jagged teeth ground together as his shoulders shook with strain, every muscle in his hulking body stretched taunt over his bones. His arousal was obvious, an enormous red cock jutted from between his legs, its tip dribbling precum onto the ground. The affliction of lust had him too, but he was holding back. Jacqueline felt a moment's confusion. Why would he hold back? She was helpless to resist him now, her body burned for him in a way that went beyond human lust, bent before him in supplication. Yet he held himself back, warring against every urge that Menzo had implanted in his head. Why?

His eyes rose to met hers and they contained the answer. Those eyes bulged with rage and lust, but deep within them, Jacqueline could see the love that was holding them both in check. Indeed, the answer was simple. He held himself back because she had asked him to.

He loved her, underneath all of that hulking muscle. With that realization, Jacqueline heard a distant drum beat. She couldn't be sure if the beat originated from her head or the forest but that didn't matter. There was nothing to fear now. She rolled onto her back and opened her legs to him. "Dave, make love to me," she whispered to him.

Golden eyes widened in disbelief, and his head shook in a wary negative, his fingers digging into the earth.

Jacqueline could not help but smile at her noble beast, his actions only confirming that this was still her husband. Even when they played rough, he needed permission. She arched her back and brought her dripping pussy right before his toothy maw. "Taste me gently, sir wolf."

His eyes looked at her askance and she nodded. Slowly, tentatively, Dave pushed his tongue into her folds, giving her a deep lap. Jacqueline moaned as the intense pleasure opened in her, a chasm threatening to swallow her very soul but Jacqueline clung to the strengthening beat in her head, finally locating its source. The sound of his heart beating within his chest.

Another lick set her wailing as he pushed his snout deeper into her folds. "Oh, yes!" her voice rumbled with approval as she felt his massive hand wrap around either side of her hips and pull her upwards. With each loving lap, her pleasure and volume grew. A second heartbeat, her own, joined with his; drumming frenetically against his powerful rhythm. His tongue, massive and long, savored her with slow steady laps, each one a little harder than the last. They drove Jacqueline wild, and she writhed and thrashed in his hands, her legs lashing out at the air while her jaws snapped at the empty air. Her heart beat faster and faster under his steady, stone-like pressure, her rhythm weaving around his like a hummingbird dancing with an eagle. With a primal scream, she bucked violently as the pleasure tipped over some invisible barrier. Overwhelming bliss that Jacqueline had never known pushed out all thought, all emotion. Jacqueline's world went white, the color of a supernova exploding in your face. She would have been lost to it, but the beat stayed with her, Dave's heart beat giving her something to follow as the bliss began to fade.

Jacqueline opened her eyes to see the forest above her, not as she had before as a dark place of shadows and hunts, but as a place of life and rebirth. The branches and leaves of the forest beat with their own slow rhythm that she could see. That was not all. She could feel the heat of the bonfire within her. It raged from a tiny mote of that bliss that had been trapped within the fire pit. It sang of love and lust.

The mind-blowing bliss had nearly burned her away, but she hungered for more love and pleasure in equal measure. She raised her head and looked at Dave, he stopped his lapping, looking at her with a self-satisfied smirk at the corner of that wicked muzzle. In his golden eyes, Jacqueline saw hunger beginning to take hold; his bestial desires would not be sated long with that bit of foreplay. Jacqueline's used the light of her inner bonfire to push past his eyes and into his own inner realm. She hissed at the sight, a snarl of tangled glamours had twisted her gentle lover. It all centered on a particular fantasy, bloated until it had pervaded his being and body, then twisted by Menzo's collar. Oh, this would be fun.

The glamour Jacqueline began to weave was the opposite of the one she used to chase Menzo. Taking a bit of the bliss-born power, she spun the gossamer threads around herself, guided by the images within Dave's soul. It started with her face. Her muzzle retracted as her lips changed from black to a vibrant red. The soft fur retreated into smooth, pale skin, and her ears shrank back to the sides of her head. Her hair grew more long and luscious than it had ever been before. The change continued down her body, the fur fading into skin, her muscles thinning as her curves became soft and inviting. Four breasts shrank back into her flesh while the two survivors swelled. Jacqueline gasped with breathless voice as the cold night kissed her naked skin. Finally, her legs succumbed to the magic, her thighs thinning as the spots faded, becoming long and lithe. Jacqueline smiled at Dave, radiating warmth and mischievousness. Of her animal nature, only her tail stubbornly remained, but judging from the way Dave's jaw hung open, she had gotten close enough to her former self for his eyes.

His want, his need for her, was a living thing to Jacqueline now. It pressed down on her glamour, correcting the imperfections, adding details she had forgotten-- like the pattern of birthmarks on her left side and the length of her toenails. Clothes, a pair of jeans and a shirt, tattered and torn from a long run through the forest slipped around her naked body, spun from the air itself. There was just one more element to add now. Jacqueline reached her senses beneath her, where she could feel the pulse of the tree roots that searched the earth for minerals and water. She listened to their rhythm and invited them to join her song. They stirred from their slumber eagerly, sending long woody tendrils to erupt from the ground around her.

The roots quickly encircled her arms and legs, pulling them away from each other, spreading her apart. She fought them instinctively, crying out with a voice much higher pitched than she remembered possessing. The strength of the roots was incredible, and soon wrestled Jacqueline into a spread eagle position before Dave,

rendering her entirely helpless. The naughty roots even threaded between her breasts and teased the inside of her thighs. "Oh help!" Jacqueline wailed with a husky undertone, "I am about to savaged by a huge beast and I'm completely helpless!"

The grin on Dave's muzzle nearly split his head in half. He growled deep and low as he fought to look dangerous. Jacqueline shrieked as he leaped on top of her and again in pain as he tore her shirt from her breasts, his sharp claws scratching her fragile skin. His huge, furry mitt clapped over her mouth, covering her entire face. She screamed into his leathery pad as she felt his talons slash away of the fabric of her jeans. She struggled and bit at his palm but found no purchase on it. The vines held her tight as padded fingers squeezed her left breast. Panic seized her, she couldn't see what he was doing, couldn't tell him to stop. Jacqueline clawed mentally at the glamour around her, but she couldn't wrench it away from reality. Weighed down by the focus of his want, his fantasy pulled from him, into reality and down into her.

He lifted his paw away, but before Jacqueline could even begin to form a word, he thrust his massive cock into her cunt like a javelin finding a warrior's heart. Jacqueline's scream tore through the night as pain and pleasure smashed into her mind. More screams joined it before its echo faded. Dave slammed his meat into her with the force of an elephant and the speed of a jackrabbit. He fucked her with wild abandon-- no foreplay, no gentleness-- giving her no quarter or rest as each savage thrust set off orgasmic explosions within her as he pushed deeper than humanly possible. The roots were torn from her body as he bit her, scratched her and held her down. "Mine," he growled in her ears, "Mine forever."

"Yes!" she pleaded with him. "More!" This was her part, the willing victim, a burning lust opening within her, matching his own. She stopped fighting him and clung to him, thrusting against him with what little strength she had. He stood and braced her against a tree. Jacqueline howled as a new orgasm was birthed with every thrust from his new position. The big, bestial cock inside her swelled as the wolfman's thrusts grew slower and deeper. His breaths began to waver. Jacqueline could feel every inch of him quiver against her walls as he pushed deep into her womb. He shuddered, then with a howl, he unleashed into Jacqueline. Hot cum flooded into her with the force of a fire hose. Cum spurted out of her around his penis, drenching him and the tree. Jacqueline's lips formed an 'O' as she let loose with her own howl of pleasure as the warm seed filled her with ecstasy of an entirely different sort. Her head lolled back against the tree's rough bark. She could feel Dave's heart against hers. They beat in time with each other

In the tree branches, she saw something that made her own heart skip a beat. Tiny hooves dangled from spindly little legs about ten feet up. In her mind's eye, a thin golden chain ran from around Dave's neck and into the branches. She let her head fall forward, into Dave's furry chest. It didn't seem quite so coarse as it had been. Her body ached and her mind buzzed from the afterglow. The implanted lust of Menzo's arrow had been entirely sated, but she couldn't let him know that. She had to break that chain first or everything would be for naught.

Another role to play. How many different roles would she need to best Menzo? She reached out with thin tendrils of glamour in all directions. One stopped and died not far away. Not far at all. Jacqueline inhaled, drinking in Dave's scent, a thick oily musk, but buried deep within it was her love's smell, definitely stronger than before. "Dave," she whispered. "I want more."

He made a groggy rumble and pulled away from the tree. Jacqueline, who had been sandwiched between him and the tree, clung to his chest, supported only by his softening member. The wolf man gave a yippee and quickly pulled Jacqueline off his shaft and set her on the ground. Jacqueline's legs wobbled and she fell forward on to her knees, only catching herself by wrapping her arms around a shaggy leg. Dave's lupine face craned to look down at her, concern in his eyes. Jacqueline met them with a dreamy stare of her own and a genuine smile. With the central fantasy fulfilled, the central knot of Menzo's glamour was gone and she could see where to pick apart the knots. "More," she said, giving her voice a child-like lift as she cupped his shaggy balls, each as large as a grapefruit.

He whimpered as Jacqueline massaged them. They were soft

and dry--glamour enhanced sex didn't stay dirty for long. The drooping cock eventually began to stir back to life and Jacqueline grinned as she teased him with her slender fingers. She licked her lips hungrily, as her own lust began to rekindle as she studied his deliciously long member. Had they slipped into another of his fantasies? Did it matter? She would enjoy this particular play for time.

She crawled forward, her tail trailing around his ankle. On all fours, she went in the direction of the crowbar just ten feet away from where Dave stood. Then she thrust her buttocks into the air, her long spotted tail lashed from side to side and then slowly lifted to reveal her red sex. "Take me," Jacqueline panted. "Take me like an animal!" The words tumbled out of her mouth nearly unbidden even as she winced at their blandness.

There was an uncertain whine behind her and then came Menzo's voice. "Go ahead boy, she wants you now. She's begging for it, just like you wanted it. Give it to her. Now." Jacqueline could feel the glamour behind that word, the sheer force of it made her tail stand higher.

He approached her cautiously. Jacqueline whined at him as he nosed her buttocks and licked up her spine, real need blossoming within her, surprising her with the depth of her own ache. Love was evident in his gentle touches, and in the link between their heart-beats. Jacqueline's loins flooded with wetness as he positioned himself over her. His fur tickling her smooth back as he placed his hands next to hers. Jacqueline mewed with impatience and thrust her rear up into him.

The tip of his cock briefly teased the lips of her pussy before sliding all the way into her. Jacqueline gasped in surprise as her walls clenched around him, like a lock gripping its key. The sheer rightness of the sensation nearly overwhelmed her. No soreness, no pain-- Jacqueline was in awe at the purity of the pleasure as he began to thrust in and out of her to the quickening beat of his heart. The plan that Jacqueline had been forming in her mind since she discovered the beat of their love almost fell out of her grasp. It would be so easy to just stop thinking, to give in to the pleasure that he injected into her with every thrust. Dave would always love her, always be ready to fuck her. What did she need with anything more than that? Dave and wonderful sex. Menzo could give her both if she was a good kitty.

She swatted the thoughts aside. She didn't need to think, she needed to move. She leaned forward a little and Dave's thrusts carried him forward a few inches. "Oh, yes!" Jacqueline cried both in victory and in pleasure. The beat was in time with his thrusts, pleasure slowly rolling through them both like a snowball rolling down a mountain. Jacqueline guided him forward, inch by inch, thrust by thrust closer to the iron that might shatter his chain. The progress was slow and halting as orgasms thundered through her, each one more powerful than the last. They had traveled perhaps a hundred feet, maybe more, when a bolt of wetness blossomed deep within her, trigging an orgasm so strong that every single muscle in her body spasmed and she fell to the earth. He came, finally, but he hadn't stopped. Hadn't even paused.

What she did know was she couldn't push herself back up from that last climax, her arms wouldn't obey anymore. They locked in place, her clawless fingers digging into the ground as she pushed back into him. A yowl tore from her throat as he pressed up into her, the tip of his member kissing her spine. She tilted her head upwards to lick at his throat as the human glamour began to fall away from her face. Her spirit soared as the feel of whiskers returned to her face and the prickle of fur spread down her back. She clenched her muscles around Dave's cock and rejoiced in the strangled growl of pleasure he made, his pace growing fanatic as he drove himself in and out of her. "Feel that?" she growled. "You're changing me! Youu'RRE!" Jacqueline roared as the change hit her hips, her thighs thickening as her spine stretched out. "DOOING this!"

He slammed down into her even harder, as Jacqueline's mind struggled to figure out why he was breaking down her humanizing glamour. Was it possible that he wanted her as the leopard? She forced open her eyes and looked at his hand next to her own, spots just beginning to shimmer back into existence on her still smooth skin. Yet his hand wasn't the same as it had been. The fur around it was sliver in color, not that oily black. Another bolt of hot and thick liquid struck her deep inside and Jacqueline roared as her additional breasts swelled back into existence, the returning sensations of her hard nipples in the brisk night air. He was pumping her full of the glamor that had changed him. She HAD knocked it loose and his body was purging it-- purging it directly into HER!

It felt wonderful as her muscles swelled and rippled under her skin, her body becoming lean and athletic. The feeling of power intoxicated her, the sexual pleasure a dim echo of this feeling. An orgasm was a moment, this was vibrant life. "MORE!" she growled at her mate, but he didn't respond. His powerful thrusts had begun to weaken. No longer did she shudder with the force to the impact, his weight on her back lessening with every stroke.

"NO! Bad dog!" Menzo's scream sliced through the passion. Dave yelped and his weight was suddenly lifted from her back, his maleness yanked out of her, drawing out a hiss of pain. "Get up, you miserable fleabag!" The voice climbed so high that Jacqueline doubted a human ear would catch it.

Jacqueline turned to find Dave writhing on the ground, large paw-like hands clawing at the collar around his neck. His fur no longer black but a dusky sliver, and the massive maw of a muzzle reduced to the modest snout of the wolves from the nature shows, not the nightmares. His body was no longer hulking, but lean and wiry. His eyes were filled with pain and they implored her for help. Jacqueline's eyes followed the chain up into the tree to the small figure within its branches. Menzo's blue eyes blazed in the dim light of the moonlit forest as he poured pure pain down through the long leash. Jacqueline hissed and dashed toward the tree, only to stop dead when Dave let out a howl that tore at her heart. "BAAACC- CK!" Menzo bleated, fixing those eyes on her. "Back, or I give him so much pain his little brain will burst!"

"You do that and you die." Jacqueline hissed at him. "Let him go."

"Oh, no. I'm the great Menzo. Royal Squire of Mab. The Queen desires a huntress and I shall deliver you."

"Bull. I know what you just tried to do to me, Menzo. I wouldn't have been much of a hunter after that. Let him go and I might not rip all the glamour from your bones." Jacqueline's tail lashed behind her as she calculated the fastest way possible up that oak he stood in.

"I gave you what you wanted. Transformed you from a dumpy little mortal and into a creature of pure beauty. It's only your stubborn to refusal to pay the price for your dreams, Jacqueline, that has brought us to t-this." The little antelope man seemed to be losing his confidence as he spoke, the hand holding the lead began to tremble. Jacqueline deepened the growl, feeling strands of magic unfolding from him, looking for an opening in her. "Do you know why I selected you to be the huntress, Jacqueline? Your very soul cried out for magic, s-so loudly begging to be something other than human that I had to answer its c-call. My only mistake is I didn't smell this one," he jerked on Dave's chain again, "on you. Without him…" Menzo's eyes went wide as an insane smile crept onto his face.

Dave started to scream. Jacqueline's legs exploded into motion, she bounded into the tree and slammed into Menzo's form.

It shattered like paper-thin glass, her paw going straight through it and her claws sunk deep into the wood and lodged there. She tried to pull it back, but the tree held on to her claws. Menzo's laughter filled the air around her, high and screeching.

"I underestimated you twice, Jacqueline. Do you think I would not learn from my mistakes?"

Jacqueline franticly pulled at her hand, but it only seemed to be pulled deeper into the tree's trunk, the tips of her stubby fingers had started to disappear within it.

Menzo's disembodied voice chuckled. "I would stop struggling, my pet. It will only make that tree all the more hungry."

Jacqueline slashed at the air around her, but it only made him laugh harder. "Where are you, you little twig of meat!"

"Safe from you." The air sneered. "You are very talented with glamour, but there are so many things you do not understand. Such as its a very bad idea to consume another's magic while they still live. Something moved within Jacqueline's torso, warm and thick, reaching up through her insides.

Jacqueline tried to think where the Fey could be hiding. Menzo had to be here somewhere; he had been real when she had hunted him. She had seen pain flash through the lead and into Dave. Jacqueline opened her sight and looked down from the tree, looking for any sign of the Fey. But all she saw was Dave, still on the ground, whimpering in pain as he clawed at the collar. "STOP HURTING HIM!" She snarled, the rage blurring her vision as something twisted around her intestines.

"You cannot save him now, Jacqueline."

"NO!" She had to save him. Had to kill Menzo. Jacqueline wanted to break his scrawny neck and taste his entrails. She reached inside, towards her inner bonfire, but only found an oily miasma of energy. Beyond the point of caring, she drew on it, pulling it up into her body.

"YES!" The triumphant voice of Menzo shouted into her ears. "That's right, Jacqueline! Use it all!"

CHAPTER 16

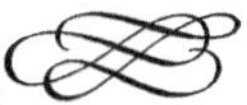

THE HUNTRESS

The tree let Jacqueline go with a scream, its bark recoiling from her touch. Her spots were darkening, growing, invading her yellow and white fur like a hyper-aggressive cancer. Jacqueline flung herself out of the tree and stumbled over to Dave, her expanding paws tripping her up. He stank of Menzo, of her quarry. She shook her head in confusion. Another scent was there, a good scent. Why would it mix with her hunted? Her hunt, her duty. She seized the wolfman by his throat and slammed him against a tree. His muzzle moved, saying something that she couldn't hear over the crackling of her canines growing into dagger-like tusks. She hissed in frustration, her claws itched to rend the pathetic dog's flesh for daring to smell like his master. What was giving off that scent? Jacqueline's nostrils flared as her nose broadened, drinking in that cursedly flowery scent of the antelope elf.

There! The collar around the dog's neck. She snatched it from his neck, taking a large patch of fur with it. The collar and the dog screamed in pain as the delicate link between them snapped. Jacqueline turned and hurled the small dog man in the direction of the iron she had sensed earlier. The stupid dog would be safe there. If he interfered again with her hunt she would have to sample his

entrails. She brought the whimpering collar up to her nose and inhaled. The collar was a piece of her quarry and it extruded fear. Yet there was an undercurrent of something else, a sour note among a sweet symphony. The sour reek of determination polluted her nose. Jacqueline's thick black tail lashed in amusement, her quarry must have a pathetic plan to save himself. Biting the collar in half, she savored its pain and grinned as it slipped down her throat. The sound of his rapid heartbeat drifted into her large, tufted ears. She would taste more than just a piece of him. Soon, she would pierce his heart with her fangs and drink him dry of his very essence.

Her tongue, long and forked, played out over her fangs as she pondered what he would taste like. Maybe she'd eat that ridiculous top hat first, then those eyes. As she pondered, her ears searched for the source of his beating heart. It only took a moment to find it. There to the north, not very far at all. She fell to all fours, and as soon as her hands contacted the earth, her hips cracked and narrowed, strengthening her legs for the run ahead. Her hands lost all their remaining dexterity, her fingers swelling into mere sheaths to hide her massive claws and her thumbs merging back into her wrists. The changes pleased her; a huntress had no use for anything but the weapons of her trade.

Shattering the silence of the forest with an earsplitting roar of challenge to her quarry, the huntress readied herself to begin the pursuit, hunching down to spring into the surrounding forest. A sound from behind her made her pause. A howl of sorts, bearing a human name. A familiar name. The huntress shook her head. It did not concern her what the stupid dog shouted. He did not matter anymore; there was only her prey now. She dashed into the forest.

The forest yielded her quarry like an offering to the huntress. He stood in a clearing, clutching a bow in trembling hands, an arrow slotted on the string. The sight of him made her mouth water, her tongue licking at the thick saliva dripping from her fangs. However, the structure of the clearing gave her pause. Over his head stood two massive trees that bowed into the clearing, their massive trunks twisting together, then spiraling upwards for nearly twenty more feet. This trap was nothing more than an insult to her intelligence.

The outline of the trees glimmered slightly to her sight, an open gate. A single step back and her quarry would be in Arcadia. The huntress pondered that. Did the silly quarry think that would stop her? Or was there something else waiting for her on the other side? The huntress growled in frustration. He startled at the sound, his legs propelling him several feet into the air before landing. Wide, blue eyes scanned his surroundings, even more intensely willing away the shadows. The huntress hunkered down into the brush.

She'd either have to lure him a step or two from the gateway or the antelope elf would have to die in one leap. Keeping low, the huntress sulked around the edge of the clearing trying to find an angle of attack that wouldn't carry her through the portal. Somewhere behind her that stupid dog still hollered that name, louder each time, and getting closer. Stupid dog! She'd have to kill him at this rate. Should have before, but why did she spare him? There had to be a reason. She couldn't remember it, but it was there; a dim twinkle in the back of her mind. Then the clanging started, sharp and metallic, it rang through the air. The fur all over her body prickled at the sound, and a spike of fear lanced through her stomach before she squashed it. Only one metal had that particular ring to it, cold iron. It rang out behind the calling of the name in a pattern, a rhythm that seemed familiar. A longing stirred in the huntress's ice-cold heart.

NO. It had to be a trick. A distraction; just noise. She had to focus on the only thing that was important. Menzo had to die. She pulled her ears from the clatter behind her and focused them on his panicked heartbeat. That tasty heartbeat. The huntress hunched low in the brambles, carefully positioning her legs to spring. The jump had to be absolutely perfect. Menzo's eyes scanned the surroundings, his gaze swinging back and forth like the pendulum of a clock. She had to time it so the first time he was aware of her was when she sank her fangs through his neck. Marking time by the little Fey's rapid heart, the huntress took a deep breath through her feline nose and launched herself into the clearing.

"JAQUELINE! NO!" The scream hit the clearing just before Jacqueline's hind feet left the ground. Menzo's head snapped back and his eyes flashed as they saw the huntress' white teeth flying towards him. He reacted with speed beyond the ken of mortals, launching himself backwards into the portal. She didn't miss, not entirely, two of her claws ripped into his belly as she sailed past him, her body curling mid air, desperately trying to get her teeth into her quarry. It was not good for her landing and the huntress slammed into the far trunk of the gateway headfirst.

A sickening crack echoed through the huntress's skull.

CHAPTER 17

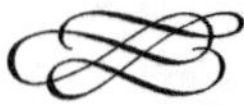

THE NAKED KNIGHT

DAVE'S HEART NEARLY STOPPED AS HE WATCHED AND HEARD Jacqueline's head smash into the tree. Naked and barefoot in the middle of the forest, Dave's head was crammed full of impossible happenings. Yet there were two things he was dead certain of, the monstrous saber tooth panther was Jacqueline and he loved her. He loved her with a certainty that was more fundamental than gravity. Everything else was unimportant.

He hoisted the crowbar in his burned hands, and charged through the clearing into the portal. He burst into a world of blues and whites that dazzled his dark-adjusted eyes.

"IRON! IT'S GOT IRON!" Dave's ears worked perfectly fine. "GUARDS!"

Something moved in front of him and he took a swing with the crowbar. A girlish shriek of terror pierced air as the whitish blot shrank back from him. Dave shuffled backwards until he felt the coarse prickle of Jacqueline's fur against the back of his legs, holding the crowbar in front of himself like a shield. The iron hummed in his hands. "Stay back!" He barked at the world beyond as the blurs in his vision slowly began to resolve themselves into human forms. At least most of them.

"What is this, Menzo?" A beautiful voice, silken and breathy in a way that made Dave think of a cool winter breeze.

"It's just a man. A bonus for you, Malady." A smaller, tan blur at her feet was the source of the second more familiar voice. Sure enough, the blur resolved into the antelope guy from the bar. He knelt, clutching his stomach. Ruby blood, so shiny that Menzo was reflected within the pool around him, seeped liberally from under his hands. "I'm sure you can find a good use for him. His passions run very strong."

"He has brought cold iron into my presence." The first voice had a hint of amusement in it, which belonged to a woman who possessed a beauty so perfect that it actually frightened Dave. Just looking at her pale skin, a latticework of lace that seemed to be spun from ice, triggered distracting thoughts that he really didn't need at the moment. "And it seems to be between my huntress and I. What is the meaning of this, Menzo?" Her head tilted slightly, studying Dave with cold, blue eyes. Dave could feel the incredible power within them push on his naked skin.

Behind him, Jacqueline rumbled and the fur against his leg stirred. Dave glanced back at her. She was laying in the plane of the portal, halfway between the two worlds. If he could just push her back across the boarder, into the real world, maybe they had a chance. There had been no audience to create a recursive glamour, so underneath all that nightmare, there had to be a Jacqueline still. Maybe Niddler would be able to help her. The two Fey were speaking again, but Dave ignored them. Carefully holding the crowbar so it wouldn't touch her, Dave knelt down. A single eye opened, and the huge, blood red iris shrunk to a pinhole as it focused on him. "Stupid dog," She grumbled at him, but otherwise did not move. Dave put his back to her chest and pushed with his legs. The tile was so smooth that his bare feet skidded out from under him with a squeak.

He gritted his teeth and tried again. "Come on, Jacqueline. Help me out here a little. We can get you home, get you cleaned up... How's that sound? I'm sorry I freaked out at the blood and the claws and *hruff*." Dave strained with all the strength he could muster, and she slipped back an inch or so until his feet slipped again and he fell to the floor butt first. "And your tongue," he panted. "Not so much into being sand papered." The dull eye watched him, but Dave thought he saw the glimmer of recognition.

"Menzo," Dave could feel the gaze of the elder Fey return to him.

"Yes, my mistress?" Menzo voice squeaked with pain.

"Why hasn't the huntress killed him yet? He's interfering with her hunting you."

"Ah, she must be badly injured, m-my Queen."

"Yet, you said this huntress was of such fine quality that it was worth all this irregularity." Her voice chilled the air in the room, but Dave still felt the lightest hint of a playful breeze in it.

"She is! Please! She the most powerful huntress I've encountered in centuries, I swear."

"Is she, Menzo? Or does your current form evidence your own weakness instead of her power?"

"N-n."

"Silence!" The command physically sucked the air from Dave's lungs, and he fell back against Jacqueline's fur, gasping for breath. The Fey smiled at him, pleased at something. "I don't think she's injured at all. Rise, my huntress."

Jacqueline shifted to her feet so fast that that Dave didn't have time to fall to the floor, one moment he leaned against her chest, and in a blink of the eye, his head rested on her front elbow. A rumbling growl vibrated through her.

"Hrrm, she is impressive." The Queen pointed to the ground in front of her. "Come."

Dave scrambled to his feet as Jacqueline stepped forward, latching onto her tail with his free hand. "Jacqueline, no!" But her long black tail just pulled through his fingers. He reached out again, trying to grab on to anything. His fingers closed around something smooth and warm. Pulling, the something came away from the tail as it passed out of his grasp. His hand clasped a ring of silver, inlaid with golden leopards. Dave stared at it for a moment, remembering when he had given it to her. The way she had danced for him. How she had bonded him. He had been so angry about the bond, so afraid of it, afraid of her. He had never stopped to notice how much love had poured through that link. The images of the pouncing leopard blurred as tears filled his vision. He clutched the tail ring tightly in his fist as a single sob tore from his throat, "Jacqueline!" The iron crowbar rang as is it hit the smooth floor, slipping from Dave's other hand in his agony. She kept walking, although slower now, and the Queen's smile grew with every step forward Jacqueline took. Dave rushed forward. If he could only touch her again, he could get through! But the Queen's eyes flicked up at him and a cruel, icy wind hit him like a truck. The ground disappeared and Dave found himself flying. A wall found him before the ground, smashing into his back. His scream of pain was Jacqueline's name before gravity slid him back to the floor.

Jacqueline still walked away, her long black tail undulating with her strides. In pure frustration, Dave slammed the ground with his fist. Ting! went the bracelet on the smooth stone floor. The sound triggered something in his brain. Something from when that black slickness had hold of his brain, and muffled everything except the sneering voice of that antelope man. Tall figures in armor were running out toward him now, pouring out of doors that had suddenly opened in the stone walls the of room. Dave just looked at Jacqueline's retreating form, and began to beat out a familiar rhythm on the floor. Ting, Ting! Ting, Ting! A single heart beat.

Jacqueline froze midstep. A single ear rotated to listen in his direction. The Queen frowned and pointed again at the floor in front of her. "Are you going to make me repeat myself, huntress?" Naked threat boomed in her voice. Jacqueline's head shook as she began to back away. Dave continued to drum out his heartbeat on the floor. To his amazement the guards stopped several feet away, gawking, as the tail cuff grew warm in his hand.

Looking down, Dave saw the he was striking not smooth, stone floor, but a rock set in a patch of earth through which green shoots were starting to grow. The tail cuff itself had changed too, the golden leopards were gone form its surface! A shiver passed through Dave. He looked up in determination from the miracle around him, and into the queen's eyes, her mouth had fallen open in shock. Jacqueline was backing away from her. Her skin seemed to bubble beneath her fur. She shook and snarled as if she was fighting a swarm of bees. The forest continued to spread around Dave, fully grown trees erupting from the stone floor. The ground in front of Dave birthed a gush of white flame. The intense heat drove Dave backwards as a fire pit opened up below the flame, the burning logs appearing beneath the flame as an afterthought.

Dave looked up again to see the Queen's eyes watching him, burning with a cold flame. Her fists balled, the joints popping with the crack of ice. As huts assembled themselves around Dave, the Queen of Winter's head slowly pivoted to the cowering figure at her feet. She snatched him up by the scruff of his neck. "SPRING! You have brought an agent of spring into my inner sanctum!" Her voice sounded like the wind howling through trees.

Menzo hung limply in her grasp, shaking uncontrollably. "I-I didn't know! Please! I just-" Her Majesty slapped him, the impact sounded like nothing less than a thunder clap. His mouth flew from his face and off into the distance. The Queen swung her arm out towards Jacqueline. Dangling Menzo before her with two fingers.

"Do you want him, huntress? I'm sure you will find him quite tasty."

Jacqueline stopped biting at her boiling skin. The blackness had begun to run off her like watery paint, patches of yellow-gold fur were starting to shine through the blackness, but her monstrous, prehistoric feline form had not given any sign of shifting. She looked at Menzo and hungrily licked her chops, her long, black tongue curling around one tusk and then the other.

Dave's heart climbed to up into his throat. The oldest trick in the book. Eating anything in Fairyland was the number one no-no they drilled into preschoolers these days. Anything included the fairies themselves. He called her name, but a wind ripped through the jungle and tore the words out of the air.

There was no way to reach her in time. Dave's eyes fell to the white fire in front of him, again recalling the bond she had made and Menzo had severed while he had mucked around the inside of his head. He could feel it in his own head, blocked like an infected pore.

Dave looked at the fire, burning a pure, cleansing white. The idea he had made an insane smile spring to his lips. Then again, he sat inside a jungle that only existed within his wife's head.

He turned to see Jacqueline prepare to snatch Menzo from the Queen's hand. As if he were watching a nature show featuring his wife, Jacqueline's bestial body moved in slow motion. She shifted backwards, arming her legs to spring as her jaws yawned open. The Fey just watched them with his huge eyes. He made no attempt to escape.

There was no time. Dave turned and drank in the flame.

CHAPTER 18

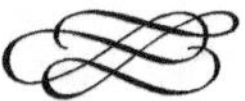

INNER STRUGGLE

MENZO LOOKED DELICIOUS. YOU COULD NOT HAVE MADE HIM LOOK more inviting to Jacqueline if you had trussed him up and shoved an apple in his mouth. Finally something that made sense. Her mind had been a war zone, the spotted leopard versus the dark miasma. But when the Ice Lady had presented Menzo, love and hunger had united once more. He had to die in order to protect Dave and satisfy the hunger. Once she had sucked all the sweet marrow from his bones the war would resume. Until then there, would be deliciousness.

However, as she opened her mouth and reached up to receive the morsel, a piece of her mind that had been left untouched by both sides began to throb. An ugly, useless link, swollen shut with the miasma's infection, bubbled to life. Thoughts started to ooze through it like pus dripping from an open sore. "Danger! Trap!"

Jacqueline froze, her tongue mere millimeters away from the Fey's boot. He was already within her jaws, all she had to do was bite down, and he would be hers. The spotted one trusted that link, while the miasma argued with its stomach. Their unity disrupted, they pulled apart from one another, separating from each other like oil from water.

139

Inside the mindscape, the two combatants stared each other down. Below their floating forms stretched the vastness of Jacqueline's body, each muscle frozen in space as the spirits drew back into the mindscape. Their war had injured them both. Jacqueline's spotted coat was stained red in several places, yet the dark reflection, a shapeless shadow with red eyes and gleaming teeth, was in worse shape. Its edges were tattered and frayed…Dave's love-beat had proven a potent weapon against it when the bliss fire had disappeared.

Still, the shadow thing was far from beaten. It grinned at her before leaping down into her body. Jacqueline sprung after it, ripping into its stinking flank with claws forged from Dave's heartbeat, but it ignored the wounds as it seized control of her jaw. It howled in triumph as their saber-like teeth stabbed down into Menzo's flesh. Jacqueline grabbed onto her neck muscles and twisted, violently flinging their head to the side. The motion ripped Menzo from the Queen's hands and sent him sprawling onto the floor.

The dark spirit screamed in frustration and hunger, as it surged back into the mindscape, streaking towards Jacqueline's unguarded precious memories and the bubbling link. With her own growl, Jacqueline took a precious second to snap the body's jaws shut before launching herself mind-ward, braving a shortcut through her doubts to cut off her opponent. She knew the layout of her own mind far better that it.

But the miasma changed its course at the last moment, springing off the wandering memory of a school bully to dive directly at the struggling link. Jacqueline's panic echoed around the mindscape, the entire world flashing red as Jacqueline realized she couldn't stop it from escaping. It plunged into the link with a splorch.

Jacqueline stared at the link. It was heading to Dave! No! No! Not again!

Yet, before Jacqueline could find a plan of action, the link gave a distant rumble. Then the scream of the miasma, growing louder as the rumbling increased and sealed link shut. Jacqueline could only watch as the infected link burst like an epic zit. The dark miasma came howling back into Jacqueline's mindscape, propelled by a brilliant shaft of white light. Jacqueline threw up the memory of her own skull colliding with the tree trunk in front of the abomination. The miasma slammed into it with the heavy crackle of splintering wood. The light continued to pour forth, pinning the burning mass of shadow to the tree. Eyes of red hate flared briefly before the creature's blackness dissolved under the torrent of light.

It was gone, but the light continued to pour in, flooding Jacqueline with warmth. With a relieved sigh, Jacqueline fell back into herself, the disparity between herself and her body had gone with the nightmare's dissolution.

Jacqueline blinked with her own eyes to find the Ice Lady staring down at her. Her face a perfect frown of disapproval. "Well, you certainly have my interest, my young kitten. However, it looks like you're not quite huntress material after all." One corner of her mouth twitched upward ever so slightly, producing an enigmatic smirk.

"What-?" Jacqueline started to ask, but she felt it before she finished her question. A prickling sensation. Looking down at her body she found herself standing on two paws, pieces of her hulking body were peeling, flaking off and dissolving into the air. Her barreled chest cracked and fell from her body like a brittle piece of armor, revealing the soft curves of her pert breasts, the last set, hidden under the plush white fur that coated her front. In the distance, she heard a familiar rhythm drifting to her rounded ears as the dirt she stood on sprouted greenery around her wide toes. "Dave?" The name came from her lips. Where was he? Jacqueline's head snapped up, and she looked around searching for him, but just saw the rapidly growing jungle springing into existence. He was here somewhere! Jacqueline could feel him, a sense of aching weariness emanated from his link.

"Jacqueline." The Ice Lady's stern voice wrenched her thoughts back to the present. She turned back to the Queen, who looked suddenly uncomfortable surrounded by a world of green.

Licking her lips nervously, Jacqueline bowed low to the Ice Lady, all those legends she used to read falling into place in her head. "Yes, your highness, Queen Mab?"

The Queen clicked her tongue in what might have been approval. It sent a cold shiver down Jacqueline's spine anyway. "Jacqueline Hopla, you have bested a knight of my court three times in a contest of will," she gestured to the pitiful creature that trembled at her feet. Menzo sat on the ground, hands clasped around his knees, face buried between them as he rocked back and forth. "As he is indisposed, the granting of a boon falls to me. I offer him to you, to consume or enslave as you see fit. Consuming his power would make you the envy of any human wizard and earn you rank within my court."

Hunger yawned open in Jacqueline as she studied Menzo's trembling form. How many times had Jacqueline dreamed of being a true wizard? His magics were laid bare for her eyes; his strength was considerable even now. He suffered deep wounds where the iron bullets had struck him and the blades of fear she had injected into him had further crippled his abilities to weave glamour.

Jacqueline turned away and looked back to Mab. She had more than enough power already-- more than she could have ever expected to obtain as a secretary. "May I request a different boon?"

Mab's eyebrows rose. "You would let him live? He will recover eventually and will seek revenge for his abject humiliation at your hands."

"Three times he's challenged me. He cannot do so again unless I issue the challenge. I need your boon to take my mate and I home safely."

"That is not so large of a boon, Leopard Lady." The ancient Fey smiled in amusement. "I would gladly exchange that little boon for something similarly small. A single service perhaps. You would like hunting with me, summer cat. I have grown so bored of my dogs." She leaned in low to whisper in Jacqueline's ear. "Imagine hunting with the moon as a partner."

Jacqueline stiffened as images burst through her-- sliver light and the sweet rush of blood on her tongue, the wind ripping through fur as red blood stained the snow. The merest notion of hunting like that, as part of the night, made her nipples harden as if they were gripped by ice. Jacqueline shivered, not from cold, but sudden warmth. "No," she breathed, suddenly short on breath. "No, thank you. Just safe passage home for my love and me. Please." Drawing herself up, she looked directly into those ice-blue eyes. "If Menzo comes for me or mine I will deal with him. Just grant us safe passage home."

The old Queen's smile grew into a cruel grin, revealing that her teeth more resembled that of a wolf's than any human, all shone with a layer of ice. "Very well, Jacqueline Hopla. I will grant you safe passage back to your original home, but do not delude yourself to think you are free of me. You have cast aside your humanity; you are part of this realm now and forever. We will draw you back to us in time." She reached up into her mouth and pulled out a canine tooth, slipping from her gum as easily as a needle pulls from a pincushion. She fixed the tooth to a tiny leather thong as a charm to a bracelet and slipped the thong over Jacqueline's head. The tooth fell between her first breasts, and radiated cold in the same way that Mab's whispers had, like sexy ice cubes. "Kiss your love with this in your mouth and you will both awaken in his world."

Mab stood back up and cast a disgusted look at the thick jungle that had surrounded them. "Go now. I'm sure Summer wishes to award you in her own way for polluting my throne room." Then, she was gone.

Jacqueline felt hot, humid air rush onto her as the sounds of the jungle filled her ears. The melody of scents mixing in her nose smelled absolutely wonderful. Best of all, one of them was Dave's. The uniquely human funk of his sweat. Jacqueline grinned and rushed into the jungle, following both the pull of the link and the sound of the drums. She ran, loving the feel of the thick air through her fur, the feel of her restored breasts pulling on her chest and her long tail following behind. Small huts rushed by as she ran into the now familiar village.

Dave's eyes filled with joy when they met Jacqueline's. She rushed up to him on all fours and then flung herself into his arms. His face was bright red as if he had sat too long in the sun. Jacqueline didn't care, she kissed him savagely on the lips, and he answered with his own ferocity. Their tongues curled and grappled until the burning in Jacqueline's lungs force her to pull away, panting. Dave ran his hands up and down her back as Jacqueline nipped gently at the side of his neck. His head rolled back, allowing her greater access while their great joy and relief flowed together between them both murmuring I-love-yous over and over until their lips found each other again. They gently interlocked their lips, his hands traveling up her back to caress her head, hers pulling his waist closer to her. The kiss broke and they stared into each other's eyes. Dave's were the same deep brown as the day that they met and held her gaze without the slightest flinch. Jacqueline wondered what he saw in hers that was so interesting.

Jacqueline deposited a kiss on his lips, and then pushed her muzzle under his chin. He offered his neck obediently as Jacqueline opened her jaws and gently ran the point of her fangs along the side of his windpipe. His body shivered in her arms and she heard a sharp intake of breath, but there was no scent of fear on him, not a whiff. She licked him from sternum to chin. Dave gave a shuddering sigh as his hands threaded through the fur along her spine, producing a soft rowl from her lips. Their eyes met again, and they stood a moment, nose to nose before Jacqueline spoke. "You're not afraid?"

His hand strayed down to encircle the base of her tail and he pulled her close as he threaded her tail through his fingers. Jacqueline could only push her head into his chest as a purr rose from her throat. "No. How could I be after today?" he whispered into her ear before nibbling along its edge. That was an entirely new sensation, one she liked very much. Jacqueline's lips parted, her pink tongue hung just beyond her lower lip and she moaned as Dave's love nibbles carried down towards the base of her ear.

"You might want to reconsider that."

"Oh?" Dave's voice was muffled.

"Yeah, because if you stop that, I might have to kill you."

"What if I do this then?" Dave leaned down, took the furry skin on the side of her neck and bit down hard.

Jacqueline's stiffened as arousal exploded through her. Her mouth opened and she cried out with a note of lust. The forest answered her with a single drumbeat that pulsed through her body. "That…" Jacqueline panted against him, "Will get you in very deep trouble."

He bit her again, closer to the nape of her neck, the bolt of arousal making all six of her nipples harden.

"How did you learn how to do that?" Jacqueline gasped as a rumbling rhythm began to play.

He released her and chuckled, "A little leopard told me. Gave me a bit of a demonstration while you were talking to the Queen."

"What?!" Jacqueline's eyes snapped open. Another leopard?! She'd have his throat! Baring her fangs she growled at her mate but he just grinned back, as if he was in on a joke she wasn't privy to. The beat swelled with her anger. Then a golden shine caught her eye.

They were not alone. Six leopard people, each seemingly crafted from solid gold sat in a circle around them, their paws beating out the now familiar rhythm on sliver drums held between their knees. Dave used her bewilderment to stroke her fur from under her dark curls, all the way down her back. The beat and the stroke were soothing and Jacqueline felt a purr rise back into her throat. There was no danger here, no malice from the drummers. Safety and comfort radiated from them, from the jungle itself. They were all part of her somehow, pieces of her mind made real.

Jacqueline looked up at Dave, her amber eyes filled with wonderment. "How is this possible?"

Dave just shook his head, "Does it matter?"

In answer, Jacqueline kissed him. Gently, she laid a series of nibbles and love bites in all the secret places she knew until he moaned with arousal. Finally, she put his lips to his ear, so her whiskers tickled his neck as she whispered. "Dance with me."

"Always." He murmured and their lips joined once again.

Jacqueline guided him down to the packed earthen floor of the village. His hands roamed up and down her body, but she made no effort to guide or restrain their exploration as she straddled his legs.

In time with the beat, she teased him, pushing herself up and a down along his body as her tail lashed between her thighs. She dragged her teeth along his chest, using her fangs to tease his nipples while raking his sides with the curved part of her claws.

Dave panted her name and whimpered with arousal under her administration, kissing her whenever the chance presented itself. Their lips met and parted dozens of time as the drums beat faster and faster, Jacqueline's movements growing ever more wild, until she could stand it no longer and mounted him, sinking his shaft to its hilt in the space of a single beat. The drums went silent and they both froze, reveling in the moment of pure connection between them, predator and prey, their hearts flowing into each other. To the silence, they both breathed the words, "I love you."

Slowly, the beat started again and the couple began to make love. They pulsed together, Jacqueline lifting herself up and down to meet with Dave's powerful thrusts into her. She screamed and yowled as Dave's hands explored her breasts and tweaked her black nipples, her own paws rested on his chest steadying her as the pleasure grew into a tsunami. They came as one, her roar joining with his howl of ecstasy as it flowed into the jungle, which answered with it own song.

They do not stop. Their lovemaking continues, fueled by love and rhythm. Twelve times they climax, twelve times they roar, and twelve times the jungle answers their call. Only then are they sated, and Jacqueline collapses into Dave's waiting arms.

EPILOGUE

COUPLE STUMBLES OUT OF NATIONAL JUNGLE, MISSING FOR AN ENTIRE YEAR

Jacqueline and David Hopla, both of whom went missing exactly 12 months ago, stumbled out of the National Jungle and into a public parking lot early yesterday morning, after a freak snow storm. Naked and disoriented, the couple was trying to find their long-since towed car when a passerby summoned a park ranger and reported Mr. Hopla for public indecency.

Sargent Rick Stevens immediately recognized the couple from the department's missing persons file on the account that Mrs. Hopla appears as a large humanoid leopard due to a long-standing glamour affliction. It makes Mrs. Hopla rather hard to miss. The MDA was quickly summoned and the pair transported to the local MDA treatment facility for assessment. The chief medical officer of the hospital, Dr. Niddler, said that the couple were in excellent mental health and is happy that the couple survived their time in the Fey realm. The couple was released this morning with a clean bill of health.

The MDA would like to remind all citizens that the National Jungle, (formerly the Kennedy National Forest) is still a hotspot of Fey activity and should not be visited after dark.